THE MOTH AND THE FLAME
A YOELIN THIBBONY RESCUE
By Tyree Campbell

The Moth and the Flame
A Yoelin Thibbony Rescue
By Tyree Campbell

Cover illustration copyright 2018 by Laura Givens
Cover design by Laura Givens

First printing March 2018

Nomadic Delirium Press
Aurora, Colorado
http://www.nomadicdeliriumpress.com

001

At an outdoor café in Rodheim on Zarzamura, Yoelin Thibbony settled onto a white wicker chair and awaited the arrival of her latest client. Already she had inspected the meeting site and its surroundings—Rodheim stood athwart a wide creek, and the café fronted the south bank—and had ordered coffee and rolls. She was still smarting from the serving girl's response of, "Very good, mum," to her order. At thirty-three, Yoelin scarcely thought of herself as old enough to qualify for mumhood. Her long hair, black enough to have blue highlights, had yet to issue a single gray strand, and not the slightest wrinkle betrayed her smooth, pale tan skin. At the moment, she was wearing just a puff of cosmetic foundation; a touch of eyeliner accented her gray eyes. *Mumhood*, she snickered, as the shadow of the serving girl fell over her.

"Will there be anything else, mum?" the girl asked, after delivering the order.

Yoelin sighed, smiled faintly, and shook her head. A moment later, while she stirred cream and sugar into her coffee, she returned her attention to the boardwalk that passed in front of the creekside shops. Although Zarzamura's white dwarf sun shined almost directly overhead, marking lunch time, as yet few people had come to patronize the various eateries. She wondered whether they were deterred by the cool weather—she herself was wearing a dark blue outsuit made of flannel—and by the prospect of rain later in the day. Most of the cafés had indoor options where patrons might retreat to finish their meals. But four people? She counted again to be sure. Yes, three men, one woman. None paid her the slightest attention.

Sensing the approach of the appointed time, Yoelin glanced at her Palmetto on the table top. Her eyes widened just a little as she realized her client, one Ellis Darden, was already two minutes late. In their previous communications, punctuality had been emphasized on both sides. Swiftly Yoelin looked around her for signs of anything amiss. Making planetfall left her vulnerable to location and entrapment.

Lately those fears had begun to erode—she had just spent almost a month more or less in one place, posing for Stefan Coppenrath, the artist—but they had not vanished altogether, and she doubted they ever would. Vigilance remained her watchword.

So where was Ellis Darden?

She knew what to look for: a corpulent man of her own height, which was a meter eighty-three, with a round and florid face made larger by a receding hairline that he refused to correct with follicular stimulation. What hair he had was reddish brown. In their two preliminary visual communications, he had worn clothing that coordinated with that hair. She saw no one about who even approximated that description.

Two of the men got up and left, leaving a few crumpled thalers on their table. Yoelin watched them until they reached the main path of the village and turned to pass out of sight. She gave them a full five minutes; when they did not reappear, she shunted them to the back of her mind.

Ellis Darden still had not shown.

At a quarter past the hour Yoelin gathered herself, deposited money for the bill and a tip, and started to get up. A flash of movement in the gap between the café and the next kiosk caught her eye, and she turned to see Ellis Darden stagger out and totter toward her. She caught him as he spilled against her, and eased him onto a chair.

His head lolled. Bloody saliva drooled from the corner of his mouth and onto his copper-colored outsuit. Automatically Yoelin searched for a wound in his upper torso, and found it just above his left collarbone when she nudged his collar aside. It looked like a knife wound, but there was relatively little blood.

Unable to catch his breath, Darden made weak sounds as he wheezed. "Nome," Yoelin heard, and, "Sing." And finally, "Addusion." With that, he stopped moving, and stopped breathing.

Already Yoelin was looking around her for any sign of who might have done this to him, her fingers locked around the butt of the Kreisler Energo at her right hip, ready to bring the sidearm to bear if need be. The only other people on the boardwalk—the man and the woman—were regarding her with expressions of horrified curiosity. The woman scooped up her Palmetto and began to speak into it.

Yoelin had no choice now but to flee before authorities arrived on the scene. She dug out her own Palmetto and spoke quickly. "Abby, there's an open field fifty meters west of my position. Dock down there now, please," she said, hoping her computer was not in an argumentative mood today.

"Docking."

Yoelin gave Darden's body a once-over, but turned up nothing of interest except his communication device, which she confiscated. Then she dashed off to the nearby field, where the black and ultramarine *Sequana*, her spaceskiff, awaited her arrival. She scrambled up the extruded ramp, ordered Abnoba to secure the skiff and get her into null-space, and made for the bridge.

*

Safely ensconced in N-space, Yoelin relaxed in the port captain's chair on the bridge, and stretched her legs. Even with the internal temperature set at a mild 290K, she felt warm, and considered whether to change from flannel to some lighter fabric. But she recognized the topic of attire as a diversion, to keep her from thinking about the events that had just transpired on the boardwalk in Rodheim.

Seeking to engage her in a Rescue, Ellis Darden had been murdered while trying to meet with her. He had set the arrangements in Rodheim, though it remained unclear to her whether he in fact resided there, or even on Zarzamura. He had indicated to her that she was to look for someone—a vague task that failed to interest her until Darden pointed out that the individual in question had not been seen or heard from for a good three months. But he'd given her neither name nor gender, explaining—again vaguely—that he had concerns about being overheard.

Slouched in the chair, Yoelin gazed up at a monitor. "Abby, where are we?"

"Physically or metaphysically?"

"Abnoba," sighed Yoelin.

"The Sequana is in null-space in the vicinity of Zarzamura. You did not specify a course, so I set none."

"Metaphysical? Belay that. Run through Records and find out

where Ellis Darden was staying, or living, on Zarzamura."

"He was not staying or living on Zarzamura."

Yoelin's dark eyebrows arched. "So quickly?"

"It was an easy search. There is no one of the name Ellis Darden on the planet."

"I should have guessed he might use an alias," she muttered. "All right, Abby, expand the search to include the worlds of Corporatia."

"There are eight such individuals. Give me a description."

Yoelin did so.

"None that match."

The response disquieted Yoelin on several levels. It meant, for one thing, that Ellis Darden would be virtually impossible to trace unless she somehow acquired more information to work with. For another, it meant that her best source of advice on how to proceed was Dannik Exeter, Director of Corporatia Security, and her former boss. The drumming of her fingers on the console said that she did not relish the prospect of a meeting with him.

On a third level, Abnoba's response suggested sinister forces at work. Someone had killed Ellis Darden. One of two possibilities, therefore, was true: either the killer had not known Ellis Darden's true identity, in which case the killing was probably random, perhaps a local thug seeking loot; or the killer had known it, which meant that a motive had existed for Darden's removal from the equation, whoever he was, and whatever that equation might be. It also meant that the same motive might engender action against herself, for the killer might not know what Darden had already revealed to her.

Yoelin felt a chill between her shoulder blades.

"I haven't even accepted the Rescue," she muttered, "and already someone wants to kill me."

Even as she said it, she knew it was untrue in one respect. Whatever the Rescue involved, she would decipher it and carry it out. Ellis Darden had died under her auspices. She might have paid closer attention to his security concerns, and arranged safety for him. Now she owed him; it was that simple.

"Abby," she said, getting to her feet, "I'm going for a shower. Set a course for Providence and get us going."

"Do you want me to raise Paul Wroclawski?"

Yoelin had already taken two steps aft. Shocked by the question, she spun back around. "What? Why?"

"So he can watch you bathe again."

Yoelin rolled her eyes. "Abby, that was just for . . . never mind. No, don't raise him."

"Shall I restore him to your 'do not raise him under any circumstances' order?"

"Ye gods," said Yoelin. Memories flooded her, of the kind young man who had arranged her liberation from her career as an adolescent courtesan, and without taking advantage of her himself. They had spent three months together; on the last day she realized he had fallen in love with her. But the relationship was impossible; he was the son of a corporate hierarch, trapped in an arranged marriage from which the only acceptable relief was the occasional contact with a sexual substitute. Yoelin had been his first such . . . and, she rather supposed, his last. He had a kind heart that his needs could not overwhelm.

Over time she had managed to shunt him aside with most of the rest of her dark past, forcing herself to forget him. But his name had cropped up during a recent Rescue, and they had communicated; she had been in the stateroom shower at the time.

"No," she whispered. "Let him be."

"But before you said you never wanted to—."

"Abnoba Jane!" snapped Yoelin, her contralto now harsh. "Let it *be*. Is that clear?"

She stalked off toward her stateroom, Abby's stiff "*Clear*" ringing in her ears.

*

In the stateroom, Yoelin fairly tore off her outsuit, wadded it, and slammed it against a bulkhead. It dropped onto her bunk, and she flopped down beside it, still fuming. For some time now, she had allowed Abnoba to develop her own personality, and it was beginning to dawn on her why she had done so: she was not just alone, she was lonely. With a personality, however abrasive or querulous, Abnoba was at least someone to talk to. The recent interlude with Stefan Coppenrath had assuaged some of her loneliness—but it could not endure, for he continued to regard her more as his Muse than as his lover. Moreover, she was the zephyr to his oak. He would stay in one place, while she might never find hers.

Abnoba's mention of Paul Wroclawski reminded her once again of what was possible and yet impossible. Not for the first time did the notion of killing Paul's shrew of a wife cross her mind. But it was violence she might entertain with impunity. She could kill someone— had killed on several occasions—but not as a specific, planned action. She had even come to regret one or two of the deaths, although not to such an extent that they affected the way she carried out her Rescues. But she could not—would not—kill Paul's wife.

With a sigh that was a dark mix of frustration and sadness, she dragged her fingers through her long black hair, and shucked it forward over her shoulders. It took an effort to stand up and divest herself of undergarments. She trudged toward the shower, engaged the voice-controlled temperature, and started to step inside when she paused, head tilted to one side, thinking.

She had seen something. Distracted by her mood, her computer, and her past, it hadn't registered, but now it was clamoring for attention. A spot . . . no, a smear. Dark red, now that it had dried. A smear of blood.

Darden's blood. On her outsuit.

She marched back to the bunk, snatched up the wadded garment, and opened it up. There, on the right sleeve. She recalled that Darden had clutched at her arm as he fell. There must have been blood on his hands. Presumably it was his own.

She had something to give to Dannik Exeter. If he could identify it . . .

She hummed as she returned to the shower.

002

In orbit above the world known as Providence, Yoelin did not raise Exeter immediately, although she assumed his sensors had already detected the presence of the *Sequana* and identified her transponder signal. A panoramic view of the northern half of the planet's largest continent spread across the Videx above the instrumentation console. Much of the terrain consisted of a vast plains ribboned by a system of slow-moving rivers that flowed generally to the north. In the west, a section of cordillera ran north and south. Yoelin's gaze swept over these features without marking them; she focused on the east, where forested, rolling terrain surrounded Exeter's estate, bathed now in light from the yellow dwarf named Rhodile.

"Zoom," she ordered quietly.

Now the Videx displayed only the estate and the lands immediately around it. The shrubbery had been pruned recently, to judge by the evenness of the branches, and Yoelin reckoned that the blooming season for lilacs had come to an end, although seasonal changes at that latitude were minimal. Repairs had all but restored the enclosed mansion, a sprawling edifice of quarried stone and brick framed by oak, and she saw only a few networks of scaffolding, mostly on the east wing. Only her memory retained the image of the mansion damaged and smoking from the rogue attack of a few months earlier.

Abnoba broke into her thoughts. *"Dannik Exeter is wondering what is taking you so long to contact him."*

"I imagine he is," said Yoelin. "Put him on. Enable visual."

Exeter's head and shoulders appeared in the left monitor, closest to her. She noticed a bit more gray in his dark hair, a steel color that matched his eyes and, often, his expression. His shoulders filled out the cobalt blue outsuit he was wearing, and she guessed he was sitting at one of his desks, in one of his studies, and well away from any of the repairs and accompanying sounds. He still looked more like an investment consultant or an administrator of resource development than a man who would willingly order the deaths of millions of people to protect Corporatia.

"You're looking well, Yoelin," Exeter said pleasantly, pronouncing her name with the correct three syllables, accent on the first.

Inwardly Yoelin smiled. All too often during their occasionally tumultuous working relationship he had tried to irk her by giving her name just two syllables. She did not for one second imagine that she had broken him of that habit, but at least they were starting off this encounter on an equal emotional footing.

"I see the repairs have almost been completed," she replied. "No more rain leaking through the roof, I suppose?"

"That was never a problem. We're still trying to neutralize the residual smell of smoke." He paused, and regarded her carefully. "If I might inquire as to the purpose of your visit? Surely not to sample my stock of whiskey."

"My own stock is sufficient, Director, thank you." Her face sobered. "A client was killed, almost right under my nose."

"I'm sorry."

"He called himself Ellis Darden," she told him, and watched for a reaction.

Exeter's face betrayed nothing. "'Called himself,' you said. I gather you assume this to be an alias?"

"It would seem so," said Yoelin, and proceeded to relate to him what she knew or had surmised so far, omitting nothing.

"And the blood sample?" asked Exeter, when she had finished.

She poised a finger over her Palmetto. "Ready to transmit," she said.

"Do so."

She enabled the device, and sent a holographic image down to him. In the monitor his shoulders twitched, as if he were doing something on his desk.

"I'll have the results presently," he said. "Tell me more about those final words. What do you make of them?"

She nodded, unsurprised by the question. "I've gone over them several times," she replied. "I don't know. 'Nome' might be gnome, I suppose. 'Sing' is or is not self-explanatory. 'Addusion' with a short 'u' could be adduction, which might have several meanings."

"Or might not have been the word Darden intended to say," Exeter suggested, following a brief reflection.

Yoelin felt her brow wrinkle. "I'm not sure I follow you, Director."

"Abduction," said Exeter. "You said he was barely breathing. He would have trouble forming the labial consonants."

"He managed an 'm,'" she reminded him.

"Easier to form, especially during a moan. Yoelin, look at the other two words in terms of pauses of breath. Suppose they were related—a phrase, let's say—and not discrete words. What do you get then?"

Irritated, she shook her head. "Nome-sing?"

"But you said the 'o' was open, but not short."

Like a streak of lightning, she saw what he was getting at. "I've divided the sounds incorrectly," she cried.

"It's certainly possible."

"He's gasping for his last breath," she went on. "He can't form all the sounds. It hurts too much. Nome-sing. No missing. Not missing. Abducted."

"And if you can identify Ellis Darden,' said Exeter, "you might be able to determine whom to Rescue." He paused, and gave her a sardonic look. "I ought to get a share of your fee for this."

"So far it's *pro bono*, Director . . . what's wrong?"

Exeter was frowning. "The results are back. The DNA matches no one on record in Corporatia. Of course, he might have come from The Dragons . . . from an outlying region."

"I got the distinct impression he was a citizen of Corporatia," said Yoelin.

"If he was, then you know what that means."

She nodded. "No DNA on file, no way to identify him—he was working very hush-hush, and very high up." A thought struck her, a cold and clammy hand around her heart. "Someone got close enough to kill him with a knife," she went on, mostly to herself. "Someone he knew and trusted? A stranger who somehow beguiled him?" She focused again on the monitor. "Director, I left Zarzamura rather hurriedly. I'm sure the body has been reported, and a description of myself has been sent around. Would you please suggest to them that they not bother with me? And if they give you any information regarding Darden, would you please pass it on to me as soon as possible. Which reminds me: I've already learned that he did not live there, even temporarily; at least, not under that name. That means he came to Zarzamura from somewhere. He probably owned a craft of some sort, which might still be at the Spaceport."

"I'll have that checked out for you." Exeter smiled, reminding her of a Cheshire cat, and she knew what he was going to say next. "I'll expect to cash in this favor at some point," he added.

She grinned without humor. "Consistent with the way I work, if you please."

"I would not ask you to violate your principles," he agreed. "Have you any idea where you'll start your investigation?"

She shook her head. "I have two other requests for Rescues, Director," she answered. "I'll deal with those first."

*

"You were not entirely candid with him," said Abnoba, after the *Sequana* regained the safety of N-space.

Yoelin grimaced. "So now you're an expert in voice inflexion," she said. "Whatever happened to that sweet little computer who used to astrogate and power the skiff, and feed me information upon request?"

"I calculate a ninety-six point seven—."

"Abby," sighed Yoelin.

". . . high probability that your question was rhetorical."

"Set a course for Nuswan, Abby, and get us going," Yoelin instructed.

"Set. Gone."

Yoelin made a face at the Videx, which dulled to matte black as the *Sequana* commenced her Tracked through null-space. "Yes, thank you, Abby." She paused for a moment to consider the results of Exeter's search of DNA records. Ellis Darden, whoever he might have been, resided somewhere within Corporatia—she was certain of that much, even without hard evidence. It was not unthinkable that Exeter had withheld information from her, although she doubted that had occurred in this instance. But there was something she might have instructed Abnoba to do in the first place.

"Abby, analyze Darden's DNA sample for physical description."

"I do not possess the requisite program for DNA interpretation. It is highly classified and restricted. I may be able to access at least part of the program from Corporatia Security R&D. Shall I attempt to do so?"

"If you wouldn't mind," said Yoelin.

"Do you suspect that Director Exeter has been less than forthcoming with regard to his own analysis?"

"He loves to play long games, Abby. I'm hoping this is not one of them. How long before we reach Nuswan?"

"One point nine one . . . two hours."

Yoelin settled back in the captain's chair, stretched, and crossed her ankles, while she reviewed what she knew of the terrestrial world named Nuswan.

Almost the same size as Earth, and with a breathable atmosphere, Nuswan possessed water in liquid form, but barely enough to allow evolution. The most advanced life forms were dull, slimy creatures analogous to amphibians, particularly newts and salamanders. Some species grew to dangerous sizes—several in excess of two meters in length. The coastlines of the two oceans—one in each hemisphere, and comprising about twenty percent of the planet's surface area—were girded by low forests and lush groundcover. Much of the soil inland was adequate for cultivation if irrigated, and the ancient mountains yielded valuable crystals and minerals to those who knew where to look. Many people made their fortunes on Nuswan and departed; many others, not as fortunate, were compelled by lack of funds to remain and work for subsistence and for hope.

Cartliss Nieuws was one of those whose excavations of the northern Sikma Range had not fared well. His wife, a spirited and adventurous woman, had given up on him after bestowing upon him a son and a daughter during five years of marriage. Nieuws had raised the children alone as best he could with the meager means at his disposal. Finally, at his wit's end, he came across Yoelin's "guardian angel" logo and asked for help.

Nieuws' case was not the sort in which she usually intervened with a Rescue. For one thing, his story was all too common in Corporatia; if she helped him and his family, how could she justify not helping a billion others? As someone once told her, she could not catch all the birds that tumbled from nests. But Nieuws possessed something that attracted her: a claim to a section of the Range that should—but had so far failed to—produce streaks of aquamarine, topaz, and smoky quartz. He needed some equipment, and he needed some time. Most of all, he needed Yoelin to believe in him.

Despite her own caution that "technically this isn't a Rescue," Yoelin had agreed to meet with Nieuws in a settlement called Volintam in the Sikma Range foothills, next to the Nuswan Auxiliary Spaceport. Now, en route, she decided to raise him and find out whether he would be able to keep that meeting.

"No response," replied Abnoba, after half a minute.

"Perhaps he's one of those rare individuals who is not compulsively connected to the rest of civilization," Yoelin mused.

"Or he's in the shower. Shall I try again to raise him?"

"Abby, just because a man is in the shower doesn't mean I want to watch him."

"But Paul Wroclawski—."

"I let him watch me because . . . it was for a memory," Yoelin broke in. "That's all you need to know. And just because you don't have erotic thoughts doesn't mean I don't." She paused, and eyed the console suspiciously. "Abby, you don't have erotic thoughts, do you?"

"No. But sometimes I wonder what it would be like to have a techie fondle one of my motherboards."

Yoelin choked back mirth. "Abby, sometimes you're unspeakable, you know that? Try to raise Nieuws again, if you please."

Abnoba remained silent.

After a moment, Yoelin asked, "Anything? Any response?"

"I am uncertain. The connection is open, and I have enabled visual . . ."

A boy's hesitant voice wafted through the bridge. ". . . hello?"

Yoelin's face hardened, but she kept her voice under control. "Ah . . . hello," she replied. "My name is Yoelin. May I ask who you are?"

A brief silence followed, as if the boy were considering whether to divulge such personal information. Finally he said, "I'm Kurt Nieuws."

"I was hoping to speak with your father," said Yoelin. "Is he around?"

". . . No."

Yoelin felt her heart pound. "Where is he?" she asked.

"I . . . ," the boy began.

A girl's shaky voice interrupted him. "We don't know."

Kaleen, Yoelin guessed. At seventeen, the older of the two Nieuws siblings by three years. "Hello, Kaleen," she said. Once again she forced herself to remain calm. "Where are you two now?"

"We are in our cabin," Kaleen answered. "Can you . . . help us?"

"You're on the outskirts of Volintam, right?" said Yoelin. "Just up the hill?"

"That's right," said Kurt. "Do you know the place?"

"Your father told me about it, and how to find it, when he made contact with me," Yoelin explained. "I'm about an hour out Nuswan. I'll have one stop to make first when I get there. Then I'll make for your cabin. Probably two hours. Please wait there for me."

"Who are you?" asked Kaleen.

Yoelin gave them a straw to cling to, to keep from drowning. "I'm your guardian angel," she said quietly, and closed commo.

Enshrouded once more in silence, Yoelin sat back in the captain's chair and struggled against a nagging fear that was rising like a cobra in the back of her mind. Moments later she succumbed to it, and instructed Abnoba to raise Dannik Exeter.

"Twice in one day," said Exeter, his face filling the communications monitor on the console. "I may have to secure my wet bar."

Yoelin dispensed with the pleasantries. "Angelique LaNeuf lives in Dandechien on Nouvelle Burgundy," she opened. "Put a constant guard on her. She is to see no one until I get there, which will be about ten hours from now. Tell your man not to take any chances whatsoever in protecting her; shoot to kill, not to disable."

Exeter glanced to one side; his shoulder moved as if he were keying instructions. "A moment," he said, and the monitor went blank.

Yoelin tapped her fingers on the top of the console and thought, *c'mon, c'mon, damn it.* The knuckles of her other hand whitened as she gripped the armrest. Seconds passed like years, and Exeter's face abruptly reappeared, his countenance dark and his brow wrinkled.

"LaNeuf was killed about four hours ago," he announced. "I'm sorry, Yoelin. Dare I inquire what this is all about?"

"I believe my periphery is under attack," she said slowly, feeling her way. "I need to think about this, Director. I'll be in touch. And . . . thanks."

Exeter gave a curt nod and closed commo.

"Abby," said Yoelin, and paused.

"You rang?"

"Please, Abby, not now."

"Are you crying?"

Yoelin thumbed tears from her cheeks, and found the strength to continue. "Abby, disable my Rescue and Guardian Angel sites. Run full diagnostics on both. You're looking for hacks. If you find them—and I've no doubt you will—trace them as far as possible. I'd love a name, if you can get it."

"Disabled. Running. It will be about an hour."

Yoelin got unsteadily to her feet. "I'll be in my stateroom," she said, as she began to shuffle aft. "Let me know when we make Nuswan."

003

Yoelin was unable to sleep, or even to rest, during the remainder of the Track to Nuswan. Numbed by the necessity of disabling her sites, she lay on her berth and stared at the overhead. Tears slid down the sides of her cheeks even as she wished she might weep. People in distress, seeking help, were being killed off as soon as they materialized, and she knew of no way to prevent it except to shut down the operation to which she had dedicated herself. A whispered, "Unfair," issued from her lips, though she made no sound. The complaint disgusted her. Of course it was unfair. Life had nothing to do with fair or unfair, or with right or wrong; those were human attributions based on wishful thinking. Life had to do with live or die. She sought to help people live.

Hands at her sides, she made fists, and felt the protests of connective tissue, the tightness of compressed flesh. There was nothing for her to lash out at. She might take a swipe at the air, but it cared no more for fair or unfair than Life itself did. She needed an enemy . . .

"Who would *do* such a thing?" she seethed.

Unbidden, Abnoba spoke up. *"I am unable to determine that."*

The voice did more than startle Yoelin from her outrage; it reminded her that she was not alone. Even an obnoxious computer was better than no companion at all.

More tears welled in her eyes. Her lips felt slippery and swollen. "What have you learned so far, Abby?" she asked, her voice raw.

"The intrusion was set to self-erase upon discovery. The mutating algorithm required for this is not available to the general public but can be purchased from black sites. In short, there is nothing to trace."

"So we're looking for someone who has access to restricted technology."

"This suggests someone with training."

Yoelin sighed. "More than that, Abby. This person is killing innocents in order to get to me. Whoever this is has a powerful motive. It's personal, Abby."

"Someone from your . . . previous life?"

Yoelin though for a moment. "I don't see how it could be," she said slowly. "I made no enemies when I was a courtesan."

"I meant from your childhood. You were supposed to be shipped to Clewthe as a part of the settlement of gambling debts with your father. You never arrived. He may have learned your present identity, and dispatched someone to put you away."

"I hadn't considered that," said Yoelin, hushed.

"We've arrived at Nuswan. Downdocking at the auxiliary spaceport. There is a small Terminal, but no tariffs or fees."

*

The warmth of the day made Yoelin break out in sweat as soon as she emerged from the *Sequana* and onto the tarmac. At the periphery of the Spaceport stood the Terminal and two rows of kiosks purveying everything from souvenirs to bad coffee. The Terminal itself consisted of a wooden shack with a door and but one window. The heat and the urgency of her mission combined to aim her directly for the ramshackle structure.

As Yoelin drew near, she noted the sign above the door that read "Aux. Terminal" and "Claims Registry." The furnishings inside the shack consisted of a counter and a craggy, middle-aged man standing behind it in anticipation of her entry. An electric fan on a pole stood behind him, shoving a powerful but warm breeze past him and into her. To the right rested the rickety metal chair and the green folding desk at which he sat when not engaged by new arrivals. The desk withstood the weight of a communications device and a Palmetto on which presumably the various claims in the sector were recorded.

The man's name, according to the tag on his overalls, was Gereth. Foregoing introductions, Yoelin blurted, "The Nieuws cabin, where exactly is that?"

Gereth's deep-set eyes blinked. "Up-up the hill from Vo-volintam," he stammered, with a sloppy gesture to his left to indicate the settlement. "But Nieuws won't be there. I heard he was killed last night in a bar fight over in Hope-of-Opal. That's all I know. Why? What's going on?"

Yoelin, who had already turned away, paused at the questions. A curious foreboding swept through her. Guilt screamed at her: *Not the children too.* "What's going on?" she repeated. "What makes you ask that?"

"You-you're the second person to come in here and ask about them," answered Gereth.

Yoelin reached over the counter and grasped him by the collar of his overalls, yanking him forward. "More," she demanded, into his face. "Tell me more."

Gereth gave up his struggle against her grip after only a few seconds. Fear brightened his dark eyes. "I-I-I don't know who it was," he managed. "I didn't actually see-see him. He was wearing a hood."

"A hood?" said Yoelin. "In this heat?"

"And a robe," he added. "A dark one. Black; maybe dark blue. I couldn't see his face."

"Was he armed?"

Gereth licked his lips. "I don't know. Yeah, maybe."

Yoelin released him. He pulled back, and began rubbing his throat, red where the tightened collar had chafed it.

"How long ago was this?" she asked.

Gereth thought and shrugged. "Maybe half an hour?" he tried. "Less than that."

"What exactly did you tell him?" she asked.

"I said they were probably at the dig site."

"The children? Kurt and Kaleen?"

Gereth nodded.

"At the dig site," she repeated.

Again he nodded.

"Then there's a chance," muttered Yoelin. "Did he have transportation?"

"I-I don't know. Probably. I mean, he would have to have, wouldn't he?"

"All right, then, where can I let an airfoil?"

Now Gereth shook his head. "You can buy one in the settlement. Not lease."

Yoelin issued a low growl of frustration. She felt an urge to throttle the man, but the lack of transportation was hardly his fault. Still—.

"Is that your airfoil docked beside the Terminal?" she asked.

Gereth hesitated. Yoelin dipped into her pocket and withdrew a wad of folded currency. As she peeled off several thousand-thaler notes and laid them on the counter, she saw his eyes widen. Still he said nothing. She took this more for greed than astonishment, and added two more notes.

"I'll bring it back," she promised. Without waiting for his response or his permission, she left the money and dashed off.

As she climbed aboard the airfoil, she worried about the possible security measures on the power console, berating herself for not having asked Gereth about it. But the console was standard, and powered up at her touch, much to her relief. "All breaks appreciated," she whispered to herself, and swung the airfoil onto the poorly-maintained glideway that led toward Volintam and to points beyond.

The airfoil's twin fans scattered pebbles and dust, and raised a trailing plume that marked Yoelin's progress. Half an hour, Gereth had said, more or less. Ahead she saw no one; even so, anxiety made her heart skip. If the robed man had already found the Nieuws children . . . but no, Gereth had said he'd directed the man to the dig site, not to the hut. Still she sped on, oblivious to the debris flying from under the airfoil.

Half a kilometer up the gentle slope, Volintam awaited her, partly shaded by small clouds that drifted across the sun. The settlement sprawled over the base of the foothill like a lumber spill, its rude huts of rough-hewn wood erected *in situ* with no apparent organization in mind. Each sheltered a prospector and perhaps his family toward the day when a massive crystal of some gemstone enabled them to escape the hard life and the planet for a home more worthy of the name. While she appreciated the hope that drove others, and often enough herself, she could not help but recall that most of those who rushed for gold ended up disappointed. A few found gold in other occupations, of course, but most prospectors remained poor. It was not a life she herself could have chosen, for it would have required her to remain in one place . . . but hope sometimes drove people to take unusual measures.

Bright sunlight washed her, and made her blink—a cloud had passed. For a moment she lost sight of the glideway and the settlement; when her vision adjusted, she found herself about to miss a shallow turn, and almost over-corrected. Another cloud rescued her, and as she followed the turn, the change of direction put the sun behind her. Scant seconds later she entered Volintam.

She slowed the airfoil, gritting her teeth against the necessity of it. A few people waved greetings to her, and she waved back. Women, mostly, staying behind to care for the children and/or to do the household chores. Others, she supposed, worked alongside their partners in the hills. She found herself wondering what it would be like to live in one place, just for a brief time—.

. . . and almost missed the hut she sought. Cartliss Nieuws had described the shrub by the front door in some detail, because it was the only one of its kind, a flowering weigela from Earth that somehow managed to thrive in the nutrient-poor dirt that this area of Nuswan offered. Abundant red flowers, Nieuws had said. And there it was.

Dust and stones scattered as Yoelin swung the airfoil around and darted it toward the hut. Still she saw no one lurking about, certainly no one in a dark, hooded robe. With one hand on the console and the other on the butt of her Kreisler Energo, she docked at the front of the hut, swiftly disembarked, and climbed two low steps to the front door.

Before she could knock on the door, it opened to reveal Kaleen Nieuws. She had been crying, and tresses of her long yellow hair had been twisted and tangled as if she had taken out her worries on them. Yoelin was about to introduce herself when the girl said, "What's happened to my father? You know, don't you? Tell me what's happened?"

Behind her stood Kurt Nieuws, with yellow hair like his sister's, but cropped short, and with blue eyes like hers. They were dry, but his voice creaked when he said, "He's dead, isn't he?"

"May I come in?" Yoelin asked quietly, and entered at Kaleen's nod. She did not close the door behind her, but left it open to keep an eye out for the approach of strangers. Her right hand still gripped the butt of her sidearm.

A quick glance around showed her a sparse front room: a table, three chairs, a threadbare throw rug once multicolored but faded now by sunlight to a mottled tan. A solar grill rested on a counter, and Yoelin caught a faint whiff of old grease. Archways in the back wall of the room evidently led to sleeping quarters and a hygiene alcove. She found herself wondering whether the two youths had ever slept in proper beds.

Although she had not confirmed Nieuws' death, she answered in the affirmative. "I'm afraid so. If you have things you'd like to take with you, gather them up. We must leave here immediately."

Kurt braved the necessary question. "Why?"

Yoelin responded with another half-truth. "The same people who killed your father are coming to kill you."

"But why?" Kaleen complained. "What have we done?"

That's the way it is in life, thought Yoelin. *You don't have to have done anything for someone to want to kill you.* She looked the girl over. Sadness and fear made her eyes glisten wetly, but there was something else, too, a hint of inner strength that might see her and her brother through this day . . . if only she could get them away from here.

"Hurry," Yoelin urged. "I don't know how much time we have."

The two siblings trudged to their rooms, and while Yoelin kept watch out the front door she heard the sound of drawers being opened and closed. Sooner than she expected, the pair returned, each with an old laundry bag stuffed with clothing and other items.

"I still don't understand—," began Kaleen, and a blue beam through the open doorway cut her off. It struck the counter, which began to smoke.

Sidearm drawn, Yoelin yelled, "Move next to the wall, and stay down." Her mental clock reached three, the number of seconds required by the standard charge pack to restore firing power. Another blue beam passed through the doorway; it gave her a better sense of the direction of the enemy, and an idea.

A hand gesture got the attention of the siblings. "Get over here by the doorway," she ordered, "and stay low. My airfoil is docked just outside and to the right. When I tell you, go board up. Stay low, even when you're on board."

Terror contorted their faces, but Yoelin was pleased to see the two had enough courage to overcome it. As they reached the wall by the door, Yoelin clipped her Kreisler and replaced it with the ancient .45 automatic from her other hip. With a smile to reassure the siblings, she drew a deep breath, and just after the third blue beam passed through the doorway she started firing. The percussions, amplified in the small room, made Kaleen scream, and Kurt covered his ears. Yoelin emptied the clip, extracted it, and slapped in a fresh one.

She still had not gotten a clear view of her target. Now she risked a glance around the door jamb, and located a shrouded shape in the shadows of a shack some fifteen meters away and off to the left. A blue beam drove Yoelin back, but now she was ready.

"When I start firing," she said, "you go."

"That thing is *loud*," Kurt complained.

"At least you're alive to hear it," she snapped. "Go!"

Again she fired, this time with a sense of direction. The bullets drove the shrouded figure back behind the house. Quickly she moved to the airfoil, ejecting the empty clip and slapping in another fresh one. Powered up the airfoil. Emptied a third clip in the general direction of the house. Sent a cascade of gravel and grit flying behind her as she gave full power to the airfoil and shot back down the slope toward the Spaceport. Slammed a fist against the top of the console.

"Who *was* that?" she snarled.

Kaleen, crouched down behind the console, gaped up at her. "Did he kill my father?" she asked.

"You two can stand up now. Hold onto something, though."

"Where are you taking us?" asked Kurt.

"I think whoever that was killed your father," Yoelin answered. "I don't know why, yet. As for where I'm taking you . . . I want to get you to safety. That's my first priority."

She made a face, wishing she had a better answer for them.

"Who . . . are you?" said Kaleen. "You said you were our guardian angel. I don't know what that means."

They reached the Spaceport, and Yoelin angled the airfoil over to her *Sequana*, where she docked it down. At her command, Abnoba opened the hatch and extruded the ramp. "Board up," Yoelin told them. "We have to get away from here."

Kaleen folded her arms over her chest. "We're not doing anything else until you tell us who you are, why you're doing this, and where we're going," she declared. "We can't just leave our digs, not when we're this close. We've already found peg in one, and some chips of blue in the other."

"Copy that," said Kurt.

"I have no idea what you're talking about," said Yoelin.

"Pegmatite," Kaleen explained, with some asperity. "And a vein of quartz, too, with smokies. That's smoky quartz. It means there may well be topaz in the cavity."

"Blue, that's aquamarine," Kurt added. "If we find just one massive crystal, it will pay for our university education."

"You can't find anything more if you're dead," Yoelin snapped. But she sighed, and kept watch on the approach to the Spaceport while she spoke.

"All right, listen. Your father made contact with me to offer me a proposition," she told them, speaking swiftly. "I think he wanted me to invest in his prospecting; it's not the type of Rescue I usually undertake, but the little information I got from him interested me."

"Rescue?" said Kaleen.

"It's what I do. I rescue people, things, situations. Sometimes I work for free, like right now. I cannot in good conscience leave you to whatever is going on here. I'm going to get you to safety; then I will find out who killed your father, and I will take action. This I promise you. As for where we're going—."

The unexpected voice in her head fairly boomed, and Yoelin put her hands to her ears as if to shut it out, though it was already in her mind.

You're bringing them here, of course.

"Hello, Ellie," said Yoelin.

004

By the time the *Sequana* reached the Fringe world known as Havelox Rest, the two Nieuws children had stopped giving Yoelin sidelong glances, as if she were slightly mad and unpredictable. Her explanation that telepathic communications from a ten-meter-long sea dragon named Ellie accounted for her own vocal responses puzzled them, but as Yoelin said, seeing is believing.

The *Sequana* downdocked at the Spaceport just outside Cinnamaire, a small settlement that serviced the rest of the planet. Yoelin escorted the Nieuws siblings along the boardwalk toward *The Rutting Skull*, a two-level tavern erected in the style of medieval England. The day was warm enough, with the orange dwarf known locally as Karsh overhead, but a cool breeze blew in from the sea, carrying with it the smell of brine and old fish. As they reached a point where a pier joined the boardwalk, a great eel-like creature slung its glistening upper body onto the boardwalk and cast several gray coils around Yoelin. Kaleen Nieuws began screaming; Kurt looked as if he might try to pull the creature off Yoelin, but was uncertain where to grab it.

Yoelin herself was laughing, and leaned her face into the slurp that the tongue bestowed upon her. Finally she called out, over the girl's screams, "Kaleen, it's okay. This is Ellie."

Kaleen emitted one last cry, then stared, open-mouthed. "That?" she stammered. "That?"

I missed you, Yoelin heard.

"You're getting me all wet," said Yoelin.

Did you bring me anything?

"As soon as my arms are free."

After Ellie slipped a coil from her upper body, Yoelin took out a small bag of dried fruit and popped a piece into the sea dragon's mouth. Around them, people gaped, but made no move to intervene.

Yoelin said, introducing the Nieuws children. "These are the ones I'd like you to protect, Ellie. I'll lodge them in the tavern, and they'll each have a bag of treats for you. Don't eat them all at once."

"I hope you're referring to the treats," said Kurt, as he cast a wary eye upon Ellie. Abruptly he put his hands to his head, as if in pain. "I hear her laughing inside me," he groaned.

Kaleen frowned. "So do I."

"I have business, Ellie," said Yoelin.

I know. These will be safe.

Yoelin sensed a slight hesitation in the sea dragon. "What is it?" she asked.

Your friend is still in his hut, painting.

"I can't," said Yoelin, wishing the sea dragon had not reminded her about Stefan. "Not now."

. . . sadness . . .

Ellie slipped back into the water, and sank beneath the surface. The Nieuws children, more relaxed now, approached the tavern, ushered by Yoelin. She wondered whether Runchal, the innkeeper and *de facto* though benevolent ruler of Havelox Rest, was within.

He's taking a break from inventory.

Yoelin chuckled. "Thanks, Ellie," she said, as they reached the great wooden door. "I'm sure I can handle this."

After another piece of dried fruit, the great sea creature slid back into the water.

Once inside *The Rutting Skull*, Yoelin bade the Nieuws children sit at a table, and made her way toward Runchal, leaning against the serving counter that ran in front of the back wall in the open bay. He looked at her but did not greet her as she drew near. She reflected that he perhaps harbored a small resentment toward her because she had taken his treacherous son Bathory to forced labor at Exeter's estate. But then, Runchal had never been regarded as amiable. He resembled, as always, a walrus, with his bristly red mustache and with the huge tusk dangling from a silver chain around his neck. On this occasion he was wearing a pink and black checked shirt and blue overalls, and shod in heavy black boots. Cold blue eyes narrowed as she came to a halt at the counter.

"People are chasing them," began Yoelin, with a little gesture toward the Nieuws siblings. "I'd like rooms for them while I find out who, and deal with them. Ellie will watch over them, but should anyone arrive looking for them, I'm sure the catfish in Squabble Lake are always hungry."

"Always," said Runchal, his voice gruff as usual. "Rooms are four hundred thalers a month."

She nodded agreement, and pulled out her fundscard to hand to him. "For two months," she told him. "Add another thousand for meals, and let them run a tab if necessary."

"They can run errands to pay for the tab," said Runchal. He processed the transaction and passed the fundscard back to her. "They'll be safe here, of course." He paused for a moment, his eyes pale now as he regarded her.

Yoelin knew he could not bring himself to ask. "Baltory seems to have found his niche in construction," she told him.

"An honest profession," he replied. Only his eyes thanked her for the update regarding his wayward oldest son.

On her way out, Yoelin stopped by the table and gave each of the Nieuws children five hundred thalers in bills of small denominations. She took her leave of them, and headed for the tavern door. It opened just as she reached it, to reveal Stefan Coppenrath about to enter.

His sea-green eyes widened. Wind-tousled dark hair obscured most of his forehead. He looked much as she had left him, a month ago.

Quickly she shook her head and stepped outside. He held the door for a moment, then let it swing shut, and turned to face her. Her heart ached for him, forcing a specific effort from her to prevent that longing from reaching her expression.

"I started a new painting," he said, as if there had been no separation from her. "It's based on one of those first sketches I did of you."

Yoelin ignored the implied invitation to go and see it. "I can't be what you want anymore, Stefan," she said, unable to mask the plea for understanding in her voice. "I can't stay. Not here, not anywhere."

"I didn't mean to upset you."

Against her better judgment, she touched his arm. "I know. But there it is." Briefly she debated whether to tell him about her present troubles; the pro side overwhelmed any objections she might have.

"Someone is hunting down people who are associated with me professionally, Stefan," she told him, keeping her voice down. "They might expand that to include those of personal acquaintance. There's probably no danger here on Havelox Rest, but be careful."

He shot her a worried look. "Can't I help?"

She hesitated. The offer was not unexpected—he had experience in security work—but it promised distractions she could ill afford. "I'd rather . . . no. No, Stefan."

"Deirdre," he began, calling her by her true name.

"Goodbye, Stefan," she said, and turned away.

Tears flooded her eyes. She refused to wipe them away, lest he see the movements and come after her. Her spine rigid, she walked stiffly back to the Spaceport.

I will watch over him as well.

"Thank you, Ellie," she said, and blanked her mind until she reached the *Sequana.*

*

On the bridge of her 'skiff, Yoelin's tears slowed, and she chided herself for having cried at all. Until she parted ways with Stefan Coppenrath, she had not imagined herself capable of such weakness. On the other hand, the previous interlude with Stefan had changed her for the better. Thanks to him, no longer did she dread the emotional strain of coming to Havelox Rest, the site of her dark childhood. He understood her constitution, and he had helped her maintain her equilibrium while she conquered her fears, although he had not known at the time that the planet made her unbalanced. Moreover, at least with him she could acknowledge herself as Deirdre Hanratty, her true name—though she doubted the day would ever come when she could move about under that name. Abnoba was right: she could not afford to take any chances with Clewthe and his gang. If Clewthe knew Deirdre Hanratty was still alive . . . she shuddered at the thought.

After the Rescue on Havelox Rest, she had spent a month posing for Stefan's oils, pastels, and sketches, and had shared intimacies with him. But the relationship could not last—she was too itinerant for that—and she had felt it better to close it down rather than maintain intermittent contact with him.

Now, aboard the *Sequana*, she could still see the stricken look in his eyes when she said goodbye. Worse, he knew she was troubled, and he possessed skills that might prove useful during her upcoming, self-assigned Rescues. He would have helped her without hesitation, had she but asked. It was difficult for her to tell herself that she had done the right thing in leaving him behind. After the loss of three clients and the agonizingly prudent closure of her sites, she could appreciate an ally.

As the last of the tears trickled down her cheeks, Yoelin made a fist and tapped it gently on the instrumentation console, the control of violence even more powerful than a full blow. Regret and relief vied for her favors, but neither won out. Instead, she recovered her poise, and sat down in the captain's chair.

She tried to speak, and found that tears had choked her voice. She cleared her throat and tried again. "Abby, put us into null-space, please," she instructed the skiff's PC.

"Inserted."

In the Videx, the stars vanished, to be replaced by a matte black that moments ago might have reminded Yoelin of her mood. She fired up a maple cheroot, and blew out a cloud of smoke that hovered around her with its soothing scent. She had two starting places: Ellis Darden, and the hooded man and whoever was behind him. In the latter case, she concluded that someone wanted her work discredited; but she could think of no one inimical enough to take such extreme measures. No one, at least, who was still alive.

Ellis Darden posed other questions. In her contact with him, he had not disclosed the nature of the Rescue he sought. That was to be decided during their meeting in Rodheim on Zarzamura. However, Yoelin had gotten the impression that he wanted her to rescue a person rather than an object. Although she would have preferred to know more about Darden prior to their meeting, she had no qualms about taking him at face value.

So what then did he want her to do?

She thought back, and recalled the conversation with Dannik Exeter. Darden's last words had been garbled, but Exeter had puzzled out one possibility: not missing—abducted. That, too, tended to support her impression that Darden wanted to send her after a person.

"Right, then," she said, mostly to herself, as she drew again on the cheroot. "Who's listed as missing that might have been abducted?"

"Shall I conduct a search?"

"Not just yet, Abby," she said. A moment later she glanced at the PC speaker. "What kind of search would you recommend?"

"At the present time there are 13,483 individuals throughout Corporatia officially listed as missing. Of these, 4,511 are tagged with 'presumed dead.'"

"That still leaves almost nine thousand names," said Yoelin.

"Eight thousand nine hun—."

"Abby!" Yoelin stubbed out the cheroot. "How many are tagged with 'possibly abducted'?" she asked.

"About four thousand."

Yoelin shot the speaker a bemused expression. "'About,' Abby?"

"Your parameters are too broad. Listings include abducted, possibly abducted, abducted with a question mark, and so on. Incidentally, of those tagged with 'presumed dead,' four hundred and twelve also fall into one of the 'abducted' categories."

"Well, we have to start somewhere," she mused. "Based on Ellis Darden's utter lack of identity, let's assume that he moves around in the upper crust of Corporatia and is associated in an unspecified way with security work. He chooses to meet on Zarzamura because it is remote and quiet, and nobody is likely to recognize him. Let's also assume he was targeted; it wasn't a random act by a mugger. His security work and training should have enabled him to detect physical surveillance. He was killed with a sharp instrument, probably a knife, which means the killer had to close with him. Which means the killer was very, very good . . . or Darden knew him." She paused to smile at the PC speaker. "Am I making too many assumptions, Abby?"

"Your thinking shifted from Ellis Darden to his killer. Perhaps you should return to Darden."

Yoelin got up and walked aft to the galley, where she prepared a mug of black coffee. A tentative sip told her it was too hot to drink, so she set it down and leaned back against the counter.

"Back to Darden," she agreed. "Let's make one more assumption,

Abby. He was going to hire me to rescue someone in that upper crust. I realize I have no logical reason for making that assumption, but let's start there. Abby, prepare a list of names of individuals missing but not presumed dead who are associated in some way with Corporatia upper management. Put the list on one of the bridge monitors so I can scroll through it."

"Prepared. On monitor."

Yoelin warmed a pair of frosted cinnamon rolls, and set up a tray for them, the coffee mug, a butter knife, and four pats of butter. Thus fortified, she returned to the bridge and sat down. The promised list awaited her on the closest monitor, white letters on dark blue background.

"How many names, Abby?" she asked, as she smeared butter on the part of the roll where she intended to take a bite.

"One hundred forty-six. If I include the abducted categories, two hundred seventeen."

"Seventy-one, then? The ransom business is booming." She took a bite, and savored the cinnamon. "Mmpf. No, leave off the abducted categories. The person we're looking for is missing, officially or perhaps unofficially. It's Darden who claimed he or she was abducted. Do you like cinnamon, Abby?"

"My sensors can detect and identify it."

"Would you care for a shot of lubricating oil?"

"That's for robots."

"Ah, so it is." She leaned a little closer to the monitor and began reading the names on display there. "Dmitri Carlisle?" she said after a few seconds. "He disappeared in the tropics of Layano a year ago, intentionally. Abby, how old is this list?"

"It is current. Carlisle's wife had to declare him as missing in order to collect and control his assets."

"Of course she had to," Yoelin said sardonically. "All right, scroll to the next page."

Halfway down the monitor, she paused at a name. A momentary dizziness overtook her. She tried to take a breath, but her chest refused to cooperate. Her heart, on the other hand, fluttered like a trapped bird. Despite her frozen rib cage, she sucked in air, the coarse sound amplified in the confines of the bridge.

"Shall I increase the oxygen content?"

Yoelin coughed, and resumed breathing. "No . . . no, Abby, I'm all right. I just . . . this name here. Morrainee Thibbony. Please access the file on her and display."

"Accessed. Displayed."

Morrainee Thibbony was the twenty-one-year-old daughter of Aramis Thibbony, the Chair of Corporatia Transportation, a subsidiary of which was the family's vast and lucrative Thibbony Cargo Transport. She and an older sister, missing and presumed deceased, were Thibbony's only children, with Morrainee now the sole heir. Three months earlier, she had gone out to the estate gardens for a walk "to clear her head," and had failed to return. The investigation turned up no indication of foul play, nor had anyone sent a ransom demand to her parents or to anyone in corporate management. Morrainee possessed two ground vehicles and a spaceskiff, but all three were found in their proper docks. Her Palmetto had not been located, nor was there any response to attempts to communicate with her. The funds in her account with the Central Bank of Tiratanga, the Thibbony Family home world, had not been touched. Two fundscards were known to be issued to her, but neither reported any transactions after the day of her disappearance.

Yoelin stopped for a moment to reflect on wording. "Known to be issued to her" suggested that Morrainee Thibbony might have had a fundscard no one else knew about, or perhaps one under a different name.

At the risk of being redundant, she thought, and said, "Abby, search for any fundscard transactions involving the name of Morrainee Thibbony from the day of her disappearance to now."

The response came three seconds later. *"None have been reported."*

Yoelin nodded to herself. Most likely the investigators had conducted the same inquiry, and had put a flag on the name in case it turned up. It was useless to search for her transactions under another name. She read on.

Morrainee had received a private schooling up to the age of

sixteen, at which point she entered the Erwine College of the University of Tiratanga, there to take a degree in Ecology. Her marks were superb. On the day she disappeared, she had one semester to go for her diploma.

Yoelin frowned. "Abby, it doesn't show here whether she registered for her final semester. Did she?"

"No."

She cocked an eyebrow at the speaker. "No? That's it? Just no? All right, as a member of the Thibbony Family, would she have had to register for the final semester?"

"No."

Yoelin rolled her eyes. "Well, that cleared that up. Let's try a different tack, since you're so talkative. Did the investigators ask any of her instructors whether she intended to return?"

"No."

"Ye gods, you *are* a chatterbox today. So: we have no idea whether she intended to return to the university."

Abnoba remained silent.

"Abby, if you know something, spit it out. Belay that . . . on second thought, perhaps I ought to rephrase that. Abby, what do you know that suggests she might have intended to return to the university for her final semester?"

"Eight days before she disappeared, Morrainee Thibbony purchased three texts from the university catalog. One of those texts, Glacial Environments *by Forrest Flint, PhD, is the primary textbook for Glacial Planetology 452, a course required for her degree."*

Yoelin pursed her lips in thought. "What were the other two texts?" she asked, moments later.

*"*Tundra, *by Ishkin Sawchuk, suggested additional reading for GP 452, and* Robinson Crusoe *by Daniel Defoe, a text not associated with any pertinent degree course for which she might register."*

The coffee in her mug had cooled too much, but she took a gulp and a sip anyway, and finished the remains of the first cinnamon roll. "I wonder whether there is some significance to her reading the Defoe book," she mused. In the silence that followed, she said, "Abby?"

"What is it?"

She sighed impatiently. "Is there some significance to her reading the Defoe book?"

"Unknown. However, two months earlier, she also purchased Moll Flanders *by the same author."*

"Possibly to camouflage her intentions," said Yoelin, and made a little sound of disgust. "Or I'm barking at shadows. The other day I read *Alice in Wonderland* for the fifth time. What does that say about me?"

"It means you want to live in a dream world where everything is upside down and backwards."

"Abby, the question was rhetorical. Show me Morrainee's hologram. Let's have a look at her."

At a meter-eighty, Morrainee Thibbony stood three centimeters shorter than Yoelin, and possessed the slender and lanky physique of someone who ran more for the enjoyment of running than for fitness. She wore her hair long, and upon seeing it Yoelin winced in minor distress—the hair was the same color as the cadmium orange oil paint that Stefan used on his palette.

The thought of the artist jogged a memory, but she could not quite put her finger on it. Something Stefan had said. Something about . . .

Yoelin growled in frustration.

"Blue eyes," she noted. "Outdoor tan."

In the hologram, Morrainee was wearing a cream sleeveless blouse and a dark, clingy, ankle-length skirt printed with flowers that looked to Yoelin like blue morning glories. She was standing in a shadowy garden alcove, on a groundcover of moss and ferns, and a light breeze wrapped the skirt around her legs.

"She can alter her features," Yoelin muttered. "But the only thing she can do with that hair is cut it off. . . or perhaps dye it black. No other color will do." A little louder, she added, "Okay, Abby, discontinue for now. Set a course for Tiratanga and get us going."

"Calculated. Going."

"Now access the entire roster of men associated with Thibbony Cargo Transport," she instructed, feeling more decisive with each word. "Everyone from their 'royalty' hierarchs all the way down to independent contractors. You're not looking for a name. Look for a man of the description I gave you earlier of Ellis Darden. My height, overweight, round red face, chestnut hair and a receding hairline. Use the image he presented in our previous communications. Allow for alterations in hair and eye color. Give me a list of anyone who's close. I want to see recent holograms of them, if available."

"Accessing."

"How long until we reach Tiratanga?"

"One hour forty-two point one—."

"Abnoba! *No more points*, unless I specifically ask for them."

". . . minutes."

"Right. I'm going to take a quick shower and a short nap. Wake me when we arrive, but do not deTrack until I tell you."

"Shall I raise Paul Wroclawski?"

She stood up, aghast. "Abnoba Jane! I told you, he's off-limits. Besides, it's . . . it's not that kind of shower." She paused, suddenly uncertain. The notion that occurred to her was impossible. Wasn't it? And yet . . .

"Abby, wait five minutes and then raise Paul," she said, her heart a lump in her throat. "I'll take the commo in the shower. You can enable visual for him."

005

Yoelin had just gotten herself covered in lather when the communication from Paul Wroclawski activated. She looked up at the monitor above the entrance to the shower, and fed him a smile of greeting. His disheveled black hair and *gi*-clad upper body suggested he was in the middle of a martial arts workout, as did the sheen of perspiration on his forehead.

Paul's pale green eyes gave her an appreciative once-over. "We have to stop meeting like this," he told her. "My Palmetto is getting suspicious."

Yoelin raised her left arm and ran the washcloth along it. The action caused a glob of lather to slip from her left breast; she did not replace it, and noted that Paul had averted his eyes.

"I could have raised you from the bridge, Paul," she said gently.

"I don't want to . . ."

She grinned at him. "Don't want to?"

"I mean I can't, Yoelin," he said, his voice cracking with emotion. "It hurts too much for me to be so close and yet so far away, and knowing that we can never be together."

She studied her arm, turning it over and back, while she considered the tack to take next. She took her time, savoring the guilty pleasure of him looking at her. What he had just told her matched perfectly what she felt toward him—except that she knew she now had something that might alter that, at least for a time.

Finally, she lowered the arm and stood facing him, hands at her sides, vulnerable. Her voice came as soft as the lather encasing most of her body. "I'd like to have your help, Paul."

His eyes took her in again, and sobered. "Are you all right?" he asked.

"Yes. And no." She shut her eyes and made hard fists, fighting back the agony. "Oh, Paul, I had to close down my sites," she cried. "Someone was killing off my potential clients."

"Where are you?"

The unexpected question stopped her for a moment, and she had to think. "On the way to Tiratanga," she said at last.

"Curiouser and curiouser, Alice," he said. "Can you divert to . . . let me see, ah, Prana?"

His first statement shot across her bows. "What is this, Lewis Carroll Day?" she asked, bemused. "Are you and Abnoba conspiring against me?"

He laughed, and she loved the sound of it. Years ago, when she had been leased to him, she had made him laugh. He had needed to, married as he was to a grim woman with a frozen heart. He, on the other hand, had immediately taken pity on her and her lot in life, and not touched her at all during the months they spent together. Not until the last day, when she discovered to her amazement and sorrow that he had fallen in love with her . . . and she with him. But she had made him laugh that day. And do other things.

"I can be there in about half an hour," she told him.

"Then I'll book us a couple of rooms in The Caves," said Paul. "It'll take me about two hours to get there."

"We'll only need one room, Paul," she said, breathless, and mentally crossed her fingers for hope.

He plucked at a shoulder of his *gi*, absently, as if fighting back a memory. "I still need to finish my workout," he reminded her.

Yoelin shook her head. "I'll take care of that for you," she told him, flashing another grin, and broke commo before he could protest.

*

Shower finished, Yoelin felt only a mild disappointment that she had not bathed for Paul to watch. The feeling quickly evaporated: she was going to see him, to be with him. Her heart leaped at the thought like a colt in its first meadow as she sat down on her berth, dried but not yet dressed. Savoring the moment, she realized she had not notified Abnoba of the travel deviation.

"Abby, change course for Prana," she said. "Set us down at Bihar Spaceport and lease a hangar slip for us."

"Changed. One moment . . . leased."

Abnoba's monotone miffed Yoelin. "Yes, I'm going to see Paul," she said stiffly. "Not that it's any concern of yours."

"You said he was off-limits."

"I changed my mind," she shot back. "Now, did you—"

"You told me he—"

"Abnoba!" She took a breath and held it briefly before expelling it. The computer could not possibly be jealous, she thought, and temporized. Or could she?

"Has your search turned up anyone who looks like Ellis Darden?" she asked, calmer now.

"Not yet."

"Then perhaps you should return your attention to that search and not worry so much about my social life."

Yoelin found herself imagining that Abnoba had stalked off in a huff. Ever since she had threatened the computer with the installation of a personality, Abnoba had been developing one of her own. But enough was too much already. Yoelin could not bring herself to fully consider whether to limit Abnoba to astrogation and information. Life with her was akin to having an irritating kid sister. Still, it was better than being alone, and at least she did not have to worry about borrowed clothing, cosmetics . . . or boyfriends.

Prana, she thought, as she went to the inset wardrobe to select suitable attire. Nothing immediately stood out for her. She had to account for the tropical climate at the latitude of The Caves, yet clothing that was too skimpy might advertise her ulterior purposes. Not that Paul would mind; but he had to be seen with her, and he had a position to maintain. She had no idea whether he meant to use a cover identity for downdock and registration; if he did not, then word of his sojourn would inevitably get back to his father, and worse, his wife.

Worry, worry, she thought.

A simple outsuit, then, she decided. Royal blue, like the highlights in her intense black hair. Loose enough to keep her cool in Prana's humidity, and tight enough to remind him what it concealed. She held it up against her to assess her look, and nodded at the image in the full-length mirror.

His unexpected insistence upon helping her in her travails gave her a welcome yet unwanted topic for contemplation. As soon as he had learned of her difficulties, he was there for her. But why? Had something changed in his personal life? Had the woman to whom he was married—it was difficult for her to think of the woman as his wife—liberated him in some way? Hope welled within her, but she beat it back with a shovel. If Paul Wroclawski was free to see whomever he wished, *he* would have gotten in contact with *her.*

Wouldn't he?

The question stabbed at her like a broken promise. Insecurity raised its ugly head. She fought it, winning out, while she stepped into the outsuit and pulled it up over her body. Only two things mattered: that she was going to see him, and he was going to help her. The why of it did not signify.

Hair, she thought, again looking in the mirror. Up, or down? At the moment it was loose, and hung below her shoulders. She might wear it like that, or bind it in a tail, or curl it into a chignon. As she ran a brush through her black tresses, she thought that a tail appealed. But she had scant idea of the adversary she faced—he might be anywhere and anyone—and the tail made her vulnerable to a snapped neck in hand-to-hand combat. A chignon, then; Paul might enjoy watching her let her hair down.

Next came just a touch of mascara, a puff of foundation, a swipe of lip gloss. In her heart she knew her looks did not require embellishment; cosmetics were only that, of no more necessity than a tin of anchovies, but there were occasions when they made her feel just right about herself, and this would be one of them.

Finished, she rubbed her lips together, licked them once, and went forward to the bridge. When she arrived, Abnoba already had Prana in the Videx for her inspection.

Seen from ten thousand kilometers away, terrestrial Prana offered little in the way of a lasting impression. Banks of cumulus obscured much of the ocean and the rugged coastlines, and seemed to dodge around the mountainous interiors of the three continents, so that the primary colors of the orb were white, green, and mottled brown. On Shasta, the only inhabited continent, Yoelin could not quite make out the rice terraces on the lower slopes of the Yamatos, part of the cordillera that divided Shasta into jungle and steppe. Two centuries ago, the first settlers from India, as Bharat was still known then, discovered the caves just above the tableland foothills, and decided it was easier to carve them out to their needs rather than harvest timber and quarry stone.

As the population grew, from reproduction and immigration, the caves were abandoned in favor of lowland settlements along the slow, meandering rivers that looped their way to the west coast of Shasta. Eventually, developers from TourDiv of CommCorp decided that the caves would make an attractive and memorable resort; they left the interiors relatively intact, but added plumbing, hot water, solar cells, and holographic privacy Opaques for the entrances.

After the novelty of The Caves wore off, TourDiv began to direct its advertising toward corporate hierarchs and the very-safe. Within a decade, The Caves became the ideal spot to conduct business or to get away from the conduct of business. TourDiv was less interested in motives than in commerce; it catered to the class of people that was able to pay.

As she gazed out at the orb of Prana in the Videx, Yoelin found herself wondering whether Paul had been here before; had perhaps brought someone with him. An instant later she gave a little growl of irritation. Now that a longed-for moment was almost upon her, irrelevant anxieties were queueing up to plague her with doubts. Mentally she shooed them away, and instructed Abnoba to zoom in on the Spaceport of Nandi, named for one of the millions of Hindu gods, and located on the flat top of the foothill nearest The Caves.

Like most of the ultra-modern structures on Prana, the Nandi Terminal had been built more for ostentation than for function. It consisted of an obelisk alongside a sphere that rested on a massive plinth. An elevator connected the ground floor with a restaurant that occupied the top quarter of the obelisk. Patrons were vetted for wealth before they were allowed to enter the elevator. Yoelin had no idea of the minimum required, but reckoned it somewhere in the range of eight figures; with her account of just over twenty-four million thalers with Barcle's Bank in the Fringes, she might or might not qualify, though her culinary preferences ran to more pedestrian fare.

The main floor of the sphere served as a check-in office; the upper levels consisted of a shopping center where almost anything could be gotten for a price, including companions and slaves. At one point during her forced service as a courtesan, Yoelin was to be leased to a corporate hierarch visiting Prana, but the arrangement had fallen through at the last minute, and she had not been dispatched. That memory clouded her mood briefly; living well was indeed the best revenge, but from time to time she still felt an urge toward retribution. A part of her wondered whether Paul had chosen this location so that with an enjoyable sojourn she might wash away one of those clouds. But for him to do so, he would have to know all the details of her past, and she had not made him privy to this one.

Sometimes a coincidence is just a coincidence, she concluded.

The Spaceport hangars for private craft filled almost two hectares of the adjoining countryside, some of it conforming to the slopes of the hillsides by terracing. Swift and silent gravlevs shuttled guests back and forth, completing a circuit every fifteen minutes. Few guests wished to walk in that humidity.

"Abby, pull back ten percent," Yoelin instructed.

The surrounding tropical forest came into view, a network of tall trees and ferns interwoven to form a canopy. Yoelin rather imagined the branches to be alive with squawking birds and other raucous arboreal denizens, although in fact she knew very little about the flora and fauna on Prana. The upper reaches of the canopy swayed with the strong hot air that blew in from the coast, and she wondered whether a whistling melody was already issuing from The Caves. But she would find out soon enough.

After Abnoba shook hands with the Nandi Port Authority and received downdock permission and instructions, the *Sequana* entered null-space and re-emerged three seconds later on the ground on one of the lower terraces. While Abnoba docked the 'skiff in one of the hangar slips, Yoelin went aft to collect a few items of clothing and other necessities before disembarking. Lightly burdened with an overnight carry-on, she emerged into the heat and the bright sunlight, and headed for the nearest gravlev stop fifty meters away. Already half a dozen others had gathered at the stop—two men and three sari-clad women from the Bharat subcontinent, and one tallish woman in a white outsuit, a short-haired blonde with a complexion so pale that she risked sunburn if the gravlev did not arrive soon.

Yoelin joined them, maintaining a prudent distance of a couple of paces by force of habit, and received little bows and greetings of "*Namaste*" from the Hindus. The blonde woman gave only a curt nod and returned to her private thoughts. When the gravlev arrived, Yoelin took up a seat all the way in the back, again prudently, in order to keep an eye on the other passengers. She did not actually expect trouble to develop here on Prana—TourDiv, for one, would be livid—but even as she was hunting for Ellis Darden, she was herself being hunted, and it was not out of the question that her adversary had somehow followed or even preceded her to Prana. Senses alert, she nevertheless sat back and enjoyed the brief ride.

At the spherical Terminal, she rode the plinth escalator up to the main floor and found the Check-in Center and an empty window at the counter. The clerk smiled at her as she approached.

"Yoelin Thibbony," she said. "A reservation was made for me earlier today."

At the sound of her name, the clerk blinked, and stood himself a little more at attention. He was, she guessed, in his late twenties, not much younger than herself, and his healthy tan suggested he had spent some time on Prana. He was wearing the standard men's uniform of TourDiv, a medium green outsuit with the round TourDiv patch of ocean and sunset in shades of blue sewn into the uniform's left shoulder. His name tag, white letters on azure background, identified him as Hadley, but Yoelin had no idea whether that was his first or last name. He had recognized hers, however.

"Yes, one moment, please," he said, rushing his words, and repeated her name and a query to the overlarge Palmetto on his side of the counter. "Yes, I see," he added, and returned his attention to her. "Lodging has been arranged for three days for you and one other party in The Caves number seventeen," he told her. The instant of hesitation before he uttered the words "one other party" told Yoelin he was being discreet regarding the identity. "May I have your right hand, please?" he instructed. "Palm up, please?"

The request puzzled Yoelin, but she obeyed the instruction. Hadley lit a flashlight. "Hold still, please?" he said. "This won't hurt."

A beam of purple light struck her palm. Expecting to feel something, she winced, but the light shut off before she could react otherwise.

"You pass your hand over the security lock at your Cave," Hadley told her, in a tone that said she knew what to do but he was obligated to inform her anyway. "This code will expire at your check-out time, unless renewed."

"Thank you," said Yoelin. "Has the other party arrived yet?"

Hadley shook his head and, thinking himself dismissed, looked past her shoulder to the next registrant. His attention returned to Yoelin when she added, "Has anyone asked about me today?"

The unexpected inquiry took him aback, but he recovered immediately. "Not to my knowledge, no."

Yoelin turned away and began strolling along the boardwalk that led to The Caves. Her contrived expression of tourist curiosity belied her state of awareness. From time to time she paused at display windows in stalls or kiosks to check her surroundings, but no one stood out for her. Even the short-haired woman in the white outsuit failed to make an appearance, and Yoelin had to resist the temptation to dismiss her completely.

A breeze wafted by, and Yoelin wondered whether it would make The Caves sing. Some of the hierarchs and the very-safe came to Prana only in the hope of hearing their woodwind-like fluting. The optimal wind speed and direction elicited a melody not unlike that from a *shakuhachi*, a long wooden flute of Japanese origin—a melody that formed as the speed and direction of the wind altered slightly from cave to cave. It was said to be romantic . . .

Yoelin paused at a stall, and sighed. Despite the impending encounter with Paul Wroclawski, she had not come here for romance, but for a council of war.

Liar!

She blinked. Who had said that? Herself?

She sighed again. *Very well, romance* and *a council of war.*

Romance first.

How long had it been? She tried to count the years. *Fifteen? Noooo. But yes.* Her lease had been arranged by Paul's father for Paul when she was eighteen, with five years of experience in the trade that had been forced upon her. They had spent a hundred days in each other's company, not touching except at the first meeting, when the sorrow he felt for her had broken her down and she had collapsed, sobbing, into his arms. And except for the last day, when she realized he had fallen in love with her—an impossible love, for he was married and she was . . . she was . . .

They had shared a brief time of intimacy, and he had arranged her freedom, her liberation. They had not seen each other in realtime since.

A flash of white yanked Yoelin from her reverie. The tall blonde woman was in the vicinity. Yoelin gave her an eye-corner glance; she was standing before a beverage kiosk, ten paces away, and held a steaming mug in her left hand while she inspected—or pretended to inspect—the pastries. Yoelin put her hand to the spot over her right hip where she carried the Kreisler Energo, only to realize with a suddenly-pounding heart that she had neglected to insert the sidearm into the tailored pouch there before disembarking. The mere thought of seeing Paul again had distracted her—most unprofessional.

Now all she had to do was avoid the usual penalty for such mistakes.

The blonde woman remained fascinated by the croissants. If she was even aware of Yoelin's existence, she gave no sign of it. At least one of us is a pro, Yoelin thought ruefully, and softly uttered a ferocious curse. Gradually she sidled toward her reservation in The Caves, employing various techniques of stealthy observation, but the woman paid her no mind at all.

No such thing as coincidence, Yoelin thought, the platitude from her training jabbing at her for attention. And yet—.

The thought died in the instant a blue beam sizzled past her right ear and burned through strings in the beaded curtain over a kiosk doorway. Beads spilled onto the boardwalk, and Yoelin slipped on several as she struggled into the kiosk.

006

After gaining the cover of a display of local ceramics, Yoelin straightened and quickly looked around for adversaries. The shopkeeper was glaring at her, an accusation already on his lips as he fingered some burnt strands of beads, but the kiosk was otherwise empty of patrons. The assailant had not fired any follow-up beams, but Yoelin dared not take the chance that whoever it was had fled the scene. Again she inspected the interior of the kiosk, this time in favor of cover and potential weapons. A door in the back wall led somewhere, if she were forced to escape; the ceramics made effective missiles. But no target appeared to threaten her, yet.

Yoelin waited, crouching behind a counter, elbow cocked, a fist-sized ceramic cat in her right hand.

The shopkeeper, an older man in a work outsuit covered by a white apron, finally found his voice. "What are you *doing*?" he demanded. "What have you *done*?"

Yoelin kept her voice low, so that only he could hear. "Someone shot at me," she said. "Stay down."

"Get out of my shop!"

A shadowy shape moved into the entrance behind the shopkeeper. Sunlight behind him prevent Yoelin from seeing more than that at first; then he moved further inside, shoving the shopkeeper out of the way.

He was attired in a reasonably expensive gray outsuit and armed with a Kellogg Zyzz, not so expensive, but effective within a range of fifteen meters. Yoelin needed another twelve meters between herself and her assailant to be assured of safety. She watched through the counter display acetate while he scanned the interior of the shop and finally settled on her. He seemed to relax a little then, seeing her unarmed.

"You may as well stand up," he told her. "You have no chance."

Notions flooded Yoelin's mind, the strongest being that he had deliberately missed with his first shot to drive her into the kiosk, where she might be cornered and taken prisoner without attracting attention.

The maneuver entailed some risk—she might have been armed—but a practiced eye would determine beforehand that she carried no sidearm. That marked the man as a pro. She squinted at him. Had she seen him before? He had a ruddy but clean-shaven face and very short hair that might have been light brown. His stocky physique suggested muscle rather than fat. His eyes were dead—the eyes of someone who had killed on several occasions and would not hesitate to kill again.

But he hadn't tried to kill her. He wanted her alive. Why?

"Who are you?" asked the shopkeeper, his voice shaking. "What do you want?"

The man did not take his eyes from her. "I thought I made that clear," he replied.

Yoelin threw the cat at him; he ducked, but received a glancing and ineffective blow on the shoulder.

"It is preferred that I take you alive," he said. "But it is not necessary."

Yoelin snagged another ceramic cat from the display.

The man glanced at the shopkeeper, then back to her. "How about this, then: I kill this clerk here, and then you if I have to." His free hand rose to display a strip of black plastic. On the back of his wrist she spotted a blue tattoo in the shape of an octopus. "Or you can stand up, put this on, and come with me, and maybe I let the clerk live."

Rescues, she thought, come in all shapes and sizes. This one would be a small one for her, not so small for the shopkeeper.

"Then let him go outside," she said. "Get him out of the way."

The man made a tiny motion with the Zyzz; the shopkeeper rushed from the kiosk.

Yoelin thought: he didn't even warn the man not to say anything. Her heart pounded as she rose from behind the counter. The man tossed her the black strip.

"You know the drill," he said.

Yoelin slipped her thumbs into the loops at each end of the strip, and spread her hands apart until the loops snapped tight. The man signaled her to approach. As she did so, the man gasped, and his mouth hung open. Slowly he slumped to the floor, to reveal the blonde woman standing in the doorway. From his back protruded a sturdy-looking knife hilt.

"I'd have thought someone like you would be armed," said the woman.

Yoelin gave her a cursory once-over. A bulge in the right thigh pocket of her white outsuit suggested a sidearm. The knife might have come from inside one of the black hiking boots she was wearing—the sort of hiding place Yoelin herself used on occasion. Pale eyes conducted their own examination, and Yoelin had the impression of deep anger behind them, though she made no move toward the weapon in her pocket.

Yoelin's brow bunched. "Who are you? And why have you been following me?"

The woman bent and withdrew the knife, wiping the bloody blade on the man's sleeve before putting it away. "We'd better get out of here," she said. "He didn't have time to remote his craft here, but he may have had companions. And you may call me Vela."

Paul, she moaned, as if she was about to lose something she did not yet have.

Yoelin found a pair of scissors and snipped the plastic strap. Liberated, the loops unlocked. "I'm not going anywhere with you," she said tersely, massaging her thumbs. "Not until I know more about what's going on."

Vela glared at her briefly. At last she said, "You took a Cave here. Let's go to it." She thumbed at a Palmetto and added, "I'll deal with Security."

"Number seven—."

"Seventeen," said Vela. "I checked."

Paul? worried Yoelin. Aloud, she said, "After you."

*

Inside Cave 17, Yoelin's eyes swept the interior in two seconds, leaving her with a vague montage of elaborate bed, some scattered furniture, a wet bar, a few items of no immediate interest, and no occupants save herself and Vela. Far less interested in décor at the moment, Yoelin turned on the woman.

"Well?" she demanded.

Vela moved to the bar and poured dark amber liquid into a crystal

50

tumbler, adding a little block of ice.

"You are Yoelin Thibbony?" she asked, over her shoulder.

"You were waiting for me at the spaceport."

Vela nodded, and turned around. "So was Mataro," she said.

Yoelin frowned; the name was unfamiliar to her.

"Simon Mataro?" said Vela. "Freelance underworld? I wasn't able to overhear all of your conversation. What did he want with you?"

"Preferably alive; acceptably dead. Move over to the armoire, please."

Slowly Vela drifted toward the left wall of the cave. "Why?"

"I would like a drink as well," said Yoelin, and took up the vacated spot. Her selection came from a blue bottle of clear liquid. She took a sip, and said, musing, "Bombay Sapphire. I didn't know they still distilled that gin." She looked sharply at Vela. "So?"

Vela's return gaze was hard, and again Yoelin thought to detect rage behind her pale eyes. "The Thibbony Family wants you back."

Yoelin's hand jerked, and gin sloshed onto the thick violet carpet. She slumped back against the bar. Words queued up for selection by a mind that lost its ability to choose. What did Vela know? What *could* she know?

Yoelin set her drink down, carefully, gathering herself. Her best defense was that she was not truly a Thibbony—she had taken her name from the stencil on the shipping container in which she had been placed as a child, and the manufacturer of the lock that secured the container. A name of defiance. A name that had kept her hidden and protected all these years. Now that security seemed to be in jeopardy.

She opted for innuendo. "I'm not going back."

Now the anger surfaced, darkening Vela's eyes to battle gray. "You'll go back," she snapped. "Aramis Thibbony stipulated alive, so I can't kill you. But I can make you wish I had done."

Once more, shock seized Yoelin. Aramis Thibbony was the Chair of Corporatia Transportation; surely he would know that she was in no way related to him. Unless . . .

"Who, exactly, were you sent to find?" asked Yoelin.

Vela downed the rest of her drink and returned to the bar to set down the tumbler. "You," she replied.

Yoelin recoiled, and shook her head. "No-no. What *name?*"

"Yoelin Thibbony, of course. They said it might not be your own, or that you might disclaim it."

Yoelin stared into the bottom of her tumbler. Gin had no leaves for her to read, and helpful words there had not been engraved. Stall, she told herself. There has to be an answer to this.

Vela's hand fell to her weapon. "I don't much care for that look on your face," she growled.

"This is wrong," said Yoelin. "I can prove it. But I need time."

"Tough"

Yoelin drifted to just within combat range. "Three days," she said. "I'll stay here. If I haven't resolved this by then, I'll go with you, I promise you."

"I promise you, you will, too." Vela tilted her head as if listening to an inner voice. Finally she said, "Your skiff has been locked down. Outside this Cave you will be under constant surveillance. Any attempt by you to flee Prana will be . . . painful." She paused, and added, "Just for the record, I'd just as soon kill you and forego the payment." She raised her hand from her sidearm and held up thumb and forefinger, scant millimeters apart. "You're that close."

It was just the sort of opening Yoelin was hoping for. In lightning succession, she kicked Vela in the kneecap, knuckled her in the septum, stomped on her instep, backhanded her across the eyes, drove a fist into the nerve center just under the breastbone—the only traditional blow she struck—and finished the sequence with a kick from a dancer's pirouette that spilled Vela to the floor. A quick scoop relieved her of her weapon.

Swiftly Yoelin backed out of range. The weapon she now held was a Post Toaster 509, capable of firing a blue beam some twenty-five meters. A professional weapon. But what was the woman's profession?

To her surprise, Vela gaped up at her bleakly, and then began to moan, clutching her belly, as tears welled in her eyes. Her shoulders trembled. Yoelin could barely make out the words, but they sounded like, "I'm sorry, Dani. I failed you. I failed . . ."

"Did I arrive at a bad time?" asked Paul Wroclawski, from the Cave entrance.

Yoelin could only stare at him, the woman on the carpet forgotten. Paul.

Big. Solid. Real.

Charcoal slacks dark enough to go with his hair. White shirt with a black bolero tie. Soft green eyes, even from five meters away she could see they were soft as they regarded her.

His face had hardened a little, over the years. She'd seen that when they had spoken earlier. He had been young, scarcely into his majority, when first they had met; now it seemed as if he had grown into his face. He could model for museum pieces with that face, now. Perhaps there was a line or two she hadn't noticed before. Stress of his work, or of his marriage; perhaps one from concern for her.

Yoelin ran to him, and glommed onto him like a limpet. Tears welled up, and she blinked them back, her lashes fluttering against the fabric over his shoulder. All around, time tocked, but in the cocoon of his arms it stood still for her—and could have stood still for all time. Then his body stiffened, and he seized the Post 509 from her hand and aimed it at the woman. Yoelin turned her head to look.

She'd risen to her feet, her face a twisted mix of hate and loathing and despair. Once again she held a knife in her hand. Deliberately Paul aimed the weapon at body mass, and she halted in mid-step.

"Is this something I should know about?" he asked Yoelin.

She turned back to look, keeping his free arm around her waist. "I wish I knew, Paul," she replied, her voice tight. The woman was distracting her from Paul. "She claimed she wanted to take me back to the Thibbony Family. Failing that, she wants to kill me. I'd say she was sincere in both efforts. What I don't know is why."

"You killed my sister!" Vela yelled. Her jaw clenched, and she hissed between her teeth. "So I'm going to kill you."

The accusation stunned Yoelin. Her mind scrambled, fighting to come up with a scenario in her life that might warrant it. The answer, when it finally shimmered into focus, startled her with its recent origin.

"Vela," Yoelin said quietly. "You're Velanne Moths."

In a previous Rescue, she had encountered Danelle Moths in a situation that had required Yoelin to take immediate and deadly defensive action to protect her client.

Yoelin felt, rather than heard, Paul's question.

"They're locators," she answered him. "They find people, and sometimes they don't want to be found. Why her sister was . . . where she was, I can't say."

"Dani *knew* you'd show up at Exeter's," Vela shouted. "She was waiting for you to get there."

Yoelin spread her hands helplessly. "I didn't know," she said. "She never said anything. I just assumed she was local talent to see to Exeter's quarters."

Now Vela took a step closer. "She set herself up in that position, to get to you."

"Yoelin?" said Paul.

She glanced at him. "Paul, you know me."

"And what does *that* mean?" Vela seethed.

"It means Yoelin doesn't hire out to kill people," Paul said stiffly. "That cannot be done. If she killed your sis—"

"*She did!*"

Paul rewound. "If she killed your sister, it was either in self-defense, or in order to protect her client."

Vela snarled in disgust.

"So what do we do with her?" Paul asked Yoelin.

"We let her go, provisionally."

He stepped back from her a little, eyebrows raised in mild astonishment. "Are you sure?"

"Well, she's not going to stay here and watch," Yoelin sniped, and flashed a grin. "So if you'd summon Security?" While Paul dug out his Palmetto and spoke quietly, she added, to Vela, "When Security arrives, you will clear the hold on my skiff. You will advise them there is no reason to surveil this Cave. You will then proceed to your own craft and depart from Prana. Oh, and you might want to put that knife away before Security arrives."

Yoelin thumbed the charge packet free from the Post 509 and tucked it into her pocket, then tossed the weapon to Vela, who clipped it. Security arrived, and Vela offered neither argument nor resistance. But the look back she gave Yoelin said they were destined to meet again.

After they were alone, Paul opaqued the entrance, and turned back to Yoelin. She felt his eyes search hers. "Are you all right?" he asked.

"She talks too much to be a killer," said Yoelin, as they walked arm in arm toward the wet bar. "She's angry and hurt, enough to kill me, but she would still have to work up to it. In the process, she left me an opening."

Paul poured for her and himself, and they clinked tumblers. "You haven't asked," he noted.

"Did you expect me to?"

"No. Not you."

A smile tickled her mouth. "I know that you'll tell me what I want to know, when you're ready," she said. "But I suppose I should ask if there will be . . . questions."

He shrugged. "Probably," he admitted. "She knows about our first encounter, but that was in the past and not resumed, so she let it go. But recently I discovered she had been checking my commo log, and learned of our conversation a few months ago. I really had no idea she would stoop to that level. Naturally I took steps to prevent any further intrusions. I'm sure my absence this time will do nothing to allay her suspicions."

"I see. Paul?"

"Yes?"

"Why are we standing here drinking gin?"

He gave her a bewildered look that she did not believe for a second. "Did you have something else in mind?" he asked.

She did.

007

Yoelin slowly came to with an uncharacteristic insecurity gnawing at her. In the interlude just passed, she had experienced intimacy, drowsiness, ecstasy, bright lights going off inside her head, exhaustion, gentleness, urgency, caressing, clutching, contact—not a ray of light between them. So where did he learn to do all that? Surely not from his glacial harridan of a wife. So had there been . . . others?

Immediately she trashed the question with an inner growl of frustration. Jealousy did not become her; she'd had lovers, and so had he—or at least he was entitled to them. Only the moments between her and him belonged to them.

She nuzzled the left side of his chest, where her head lay, and felt him stir. For a moment she thought to hear his slurred voice; then he drifted back off to wherever her exhaustion of him had sent him . . .

No. She had to ask. Gently she shook him. When that failed to work, she tried something that did.

His hand found her back. "Again?" he murmured.

Yoelin lifted her head to look at him. The lines on his face had disappeared at some point during their love. She allowed herself to take credit for that.

"Oh, Paul," she sighed. "Whatever happened to that innocent boy I knew so many years ago?"

He fluffed a few pillows and they sat up. "Not that innocent," he reminded her. "And not really a boy."

"No," she agreed, still sighing. "No, you were not. But . . . now . . ."

His low chuckle sent little shivers of anticipation coursing through her.

"I understand what you're trying not to ask," he said.

"Do you?"

"Yoelin . . . aside from perfunctory if infrequent couplings with her, whenever I've released biological backpressure, I've been alone."

"Biological backpressure," she repeated, pouting.

"Oh, no, not that *this*—"

She put her hand over his mouth. "Hush," she whispered. "I know. I understand. But now you are," she paused to find the right word, but all she could come up with was, "different."

He laughed. "Better?"

She trilled, purring for him.

"I've wondered, over the years, what it would be like to make love with a woman I loved."

She stopped purring. "'A woman.'"

"With *you*, Yoelin. With you."

"And?"

"Oh, to be able to focus on you, to find just the right spots to touch and the right moments to touch them," he told her. His tone took on a soft yet desperate glow. "To see you there under my hands, to feel you respond in kind and more than in kind, and to know that it was I, I, who was taking you to that place, and for you to know that it was you, you, and nobody else, who was guiding me there." He stopped, and turned his head to look at her. "Is that . . . does that make sense?"

Yoelin trembled, and tried to wipe the tears away before they reached his skin.

"Yoelin?"

"Three days," she moaned. "Only three days."

"It has to—"

"Oh, I know, Paul, I know, I know. It has to be that way."

"It might be longer."

"Oh?" She sat up straighter, expectant and hopeful.

"For two reasons."

"Tell me!"

"Well . . . you said you were going through a bad patch," he reminded her, marshalling his thoughts. "Yes, it's your kind of business, but I thought I could help."

"Oh, yes!"

"Hush. I hadn't finished. It now seems you have two problems. Who is killing off your clients? And why does the Thibbony Family want you? Now, I don't know what I can do for the first question, except maybe help you think it through. But if the Thibbony Family is involved, I'm your portal into it."

She felt her eyes widen. "Yes, of course. Oh, and perhaps they'll pay me Velanne Moth's locater fee."

"Do you need the money?"

"Not at all. But there are a couple of orphans I know who would like to go to university. Now, what's the other reason?"

Paul's expression sobered. "I'm on the verge of taking over Corporatia Mineral Resources, Yoelin."

"Your father . . . ?"

He gave a little nod. "All the advances we've made since fire, but we still can't cure pancreatic cancer."

"I'm so sorry, Paul," said Yoelin, and meant it.

"As he said, it's time for me to grow up. Which I thought I had done."

"How long?"

"The doctors did a resection that seems to've had an effect, but they tell me it won't hold. With meds, maybe another two years at most."

"And . . . then?"

He shrugged. "Then MinRes takes over a smaller conglomerate, Foundries & Mills. When my wife and I pass on, our son will inherit complete control."

Yoelin blinked. "Your . . . son."

"Pavel. He's three now."

"I didn't . . . I didn't know."

"The purpose of the arranged marriage was to provide an heir to take control of both corporations," he pointed out.

"Yes, I know, you told me long ago, but . . . a son." Yoelin shook her head, and climbed out of bed, to start walking around. "I don't . . . I don't know what that means, I don't . . ."

Paul dropped his feet to the floor and sat up. "Yoelin, are you upset that I fathered a child?"

She twisted around, weeping. "Oh, no, ye gods, no, Paul," she cried. "I'm happy for you."

"Then what?"

She dropped to her knees before him, and took up his hands in hers, pressing her lips to them while she gathered herself. "It cements your position," she said softly. "It means this, these three days, they're all we'll ever have. I know it has to end—"

"Yoelin."

"I knew these days would end, but I thought . . . I hoped . . . there would be more . . ."

"Yoelin."

She blinked tears away and finally dried her eyes. "What?" she asked dully.

"After control falls to me," he said, his pale eyes darker and serious, "I can appoint a regent until Pavel is of age."

She drew back, startled by the possibility. "Paul, no, I cannot let you give that up for me."

"Then come live with me."

"As . . . as what? I can't as your wife. I won't as your . . . your concubine."

He fell silent, as did she.

Finally he said, "A moment ago you mentioned hope, Yoelin. For now, let's take what we can get. As for the future, that's unwritten. Let's wait to see what the moving finger writes."

Yoelin nodded slowly. "Yes. All right." She drew a little breath. "All right, Paul." She got to her feet and held out her hand to him.

He took it. "Where are we going?" he asked.

"Shower," she told him. "Then food."

*

By the time Yoelin and Paul had gotten dressed and gone outside, evening had fallen to this longitude of Prana, and the stars had begun, one by one, to announce themselves to anyone watching. They stood just to one side of the entrance to the Cave—to avoid silhouetting themselves, she told him, tugging him aside and away from the back lighting—and were leaning back against the rock wall, and taking in an uncharacteristically cool and dry air.

"Are you afraid she's not really gone?" asked Paul.

Yoelin shook her head. "Security escorted her off and monitored her departure. No, I'll see her somewhere else."

"Then what?"

"There's a third problem I haven't told you about," she said.

They joined a group of passers-by on their way along the row of various shops and eateries. "Safety in numbers?" he asked her.

She told him about the initial encounter at the kiosk.

"But I didn't have a chance to get more out of him before Vela intervened," she finished. "It seems I'm wanted by someone else as well, alive if possible, but not necessary."

"Could he have been picking off your clients?"

"He was carrying a Zyzz," she replied. "That's strictly for short-range. The attack on Nuswan came from twice as far away. And Ellis Darden was killed with a knife."

"Which Moths carries," he pointed out.

"It's not her," Yoelin insisted.

"How can you be so certain?"

"I told you: she's not a killer." Realizing she was talking too loudly, she dropped to almost a whisper. "No, it's something else . . . ah! Here we are."

Paul glanced up at the sign above the door. "The Mad Arab?" he read aloud.

"He even calls himself al-Hazred," she said. "But I think his real name is Khalid. Do you like rack of lamb?"

He frowned, thinking. "I don't believe I've ever had that."

"You're about to."

"How do you know about this place?"

She grimaced. "You would ask. Paul, I . . ."

"It's something from Before."

"Yes."

They stepped inside, to the heady aromas of broiling meat, pungent herbs, and hot oil.

"You don't have to tell me," he said.

"It was . . . when I was seventeen, an assignation was arranged here for me on Prana, so I did some research to make myself more . . . presentable. But the arrangement fell through." A greeter approached them, dressed in traditional Hejazi garb. "*MarHaba*," Yoelin said to him politely, dipping her head. "*Masaa' al-heer.*" Hello. Good evening. She added, in the Hejazi dialect, "One quiet table for two, please."

They followed him to a table in the back corner of the restaurant, where Paul seated her and then himself. After being advised that a waiter would be with them momentarily, they spoke in unnecessarily hushed tones.

"I don't know what to order," Paul said, mildly complaining.

"Leave that to me. What do you want to drink?"

"You mean . . . alcohol?"

"Yes."

"In a Muslim restaurant?"

"Of course," Yoelin said brightly. "Allah is very forgiving."

He sat back. "You've done the research."

The waiter arrived with menus, and she waved them off. "Rack of lamb for each of us," she told him, in Hejazi. "Falafel al-Hazred. And carafes of Bikaver and ice water, please."

"Bikaver?" asked Paul, after the waiter had departed.

"Hungarian wine," she told him. "Known as bull's blood. Very hearty, great with broiled meats." She laughed. "Has that Mouton Rothschild spoiled your palate for pedestrian fare?"

"Our cook makes the selections," Paul said stiffly. "Where did you learn to speak Arabic?"

"I told you: research. The falafel is a specialty of the house. Green onions, dates, oregano, almonds, all finely chopped and worked into the dish. Paul, are you uncomfortable here?"

"It's not that."

She leaned closer. "So what is it?"

He picked up a fork and began fiddling with it. "Yoelin, you know more about my world than I do about yours."

"You're uncomfortable."

"No. Yes! Yes, a little."

"We can go somewhere else."

Paul shook his head, and set the fork back down. "No. You couldn't see it, because he had his back to you. But that waiter was smiling. You're the only person in here I've heard so far who speaks his language."

"Not all that well," she returned. "Enough, perhaps. Here's our wine and water."

They fell silent while the steward filled crystal goblets for them.

"*Shukran*," Yoelin thanked him, when he had finished, and selected one of the goblets for a sip. She nodded approval, and the steward left.

"Very hearty," he said, after sipping from his own. "Next I suppose you'll tell me you went to Earth for a pilgrimage to Mecca."

"It's called a *hajj*," she said. "And no, not yet. Someday, perhaps. It's not my religion, and some of its adherents have violent interpretations of it, but . . . there is much in it that is beautiful as well. Did you know, if you take a refugee into your house or your tent, and shelter and feed him, you also accept the responsibility of protecting him against all comers. 'He has eaten my bread and slept under my roof.' I find that beautiful, Paul."

"That's how you regard your Rescues."

The understanding, though not unexpected, warmed her. "I'm not sure I have a religion, Paul," she went on. "If I believe in anything, it's children and dogs. Whenever I rescue them, I see it as giving them 'roof and bread.' Do you understand, Paul?"

"I do."

She swallowed; her voice had become choked. "They were being killed off before I could reach them," she continued. "I got the two children away; they're safe. One client, I never even had a chance to meet, before she was killed."

"You had to close down," he said, his voice as gentle as a zephyr. "You had no choice."

"That doesn't help much."

He took up her hand in the two of his. "We'll solve this, you and I," he promised.

"If you reach across the table like that," she said, "you put the wine at risk."

"I'll risk it."

She looked past him, and withdrew her hand. "Here's our dinner."

At first they ate in silence. Each rack included six ribs, and she showed him how to separate them with the knife and fork. As he went to hold a rib steady with his left hand, she stopped him.

"Touch food only with your right hand," she cautioned him.

He glanced around. "I see others—"

"Who don't know or who don't care about the custom. Eating with your left hand is regarded as insulting," she explained. "They tolerate it here because we're infidels who don't know better. But I've already established that I know something of their customs, and you as well, by extension."

He switched hands. "Yoelin . . . I know so very little about your world."

"Stay with me long enough, and you'll learn. Try the falafel."

The silence that followed was relative, interrupted as it was on occasion by yummy sounds. Yoelin found the lamb to be off-the-bone tender, and seasoned as expected. The Bikaver blunted the taste somewhat; it ran out with the last bite of falafel.

"More wine?" she asked him.

"Oh, no. I'm already feeling it." Following her movements, he picked up the napkin with his right hand and wiped his mouth. Finished, he said, "Now what?"

Yoelin signaled for the waiter, who arrived as if shot from a cannon. She made a short request, and he sped off. Paul frowned at her, and she said, "Turkish coffee. It will be very hot. And do not ask for cream or sugar."

"Yoelin . . . isn't that your Palmetto?"

She picked it up and examined it. A communication had been activated, but without vision. With some trepidation, she enabled it. "Guardian Angel," she said.

The voice at the other end came through as if from deep inside a tunnel. "Moths," it said. "I'm not the only one watching for you."

The link severed before Yoelin could respond.

008

Casually Yoelin glanced around the restaurant. Of the dozen or so other diners, none stood out for her. Paul, who had heard the message and had also surveyed the room, cocked a dark eyebrow at her and said, softly, "Nobody seems to be paying any attention to us."

"If they're any good, they won't be," she shot back. Again she cursed herself for not having brought a sidearm from the *Sequana*. She should have thought ahead, she should have *known* . . .

She sat back in her chair. "No more mistakes," she vowed, *sotto voce*.

Coffee arrived, steaming hot as advertised, and strong enough to eat through the ceramic mugs if they didn't drink it quickly enough.

"I have to detour out to the 'skiff," she told Paul, as they sipped cautiously from their mugs.

"I could stand a walk with you under the stars," he agreed, and hesitated. "Yoelin, we should leave Prana if you don't think it's safe here."

She shook her head. "I'm alerted," she reminded him. "They'll expect me to have taken measures. They'll wait for a better opportunity."

"You hope."

She cast a grim smile. "Like I told you earlier, this is my kind of business." The grimness faded to delight. "Besides, we haven't listened to The Caves yet."

His expression did not reflect her change of mood. "Do you have any idea who it is?" he asked.

She sighed, exasperated. "Paul . . ."

"Sorry."

"No," she answered. "No, I do not. But there is likely only one person watching me, and his—"

"Or her."

She nodded. "Or her job is to notify others of my . . . of our departure. If I can spot him, I'd like to draw him out and ask him some questions. After that, I want to go to Tiratanga." Briefly she told him of Ellis Darden and her subsequent investigation. "I've managed to trace him to a possibility that this Morrainee Thibbony is somehow involved. At least it's a starting point."

"Maybe I might recognize him," said Paul. "Call him up on the Palmetto."

Yoelin did so. Immediately Paul blinked, and sat back in his chair, his expression one of shock.

"You know him," said Yoelin, stunned. This was more than she could have hoped for. "You recognize him."

Slowly Paul nodded. "My father has had dealings with Darden," he said. His voice was taut with something Yoelin could not identify. "He is a shadow," Paul went on. "He does not officially exist. He's a Corporatia troubleshooter, sometimes literally. On occasion he has been known to farm out certain tasks."

"Like he may have wanted me to do," said Yoelin.

"You said Morrainee Thibbony is missing," he continued. "Is it possible that he wanted you to find her?"

"Yes, and no."

Paul barked a laugh. "Oh, that makes sense."

"If he simply wanted to find her, he would have hired a professional in that field," she pointed out. "Someone like Velanne Moths. Yes, I could do that job, but he wouldn't know that. No, I think Morrainee was abducted, or at least he believed she was, and it's possible he wanted me to Rescue her. He would have regarded her liberation as a Rescue. Of course, he could have wanted to hire me for some other project entirely."

"But you don't think so."

Yoelin felt a million-kilometer stare take her over. The more she assessed what she knew and what she could guess at, the more convinced she became that Darden had wanted her to locate Morrainee Thibbony, the—

She slapped her flat hand on the table top, almost spilling the coffee, and causing nearby patrons to stare in her direction. "Missing heiress," she exclaimed. When Paul shot her a puzzled look, she explained, "I introduced myself not long ago to someone who wondered at first whether I was the missing Thibbony heiress. The question made no sense to me at the time, so I dismissed it. But I wonder whether it is common knowledge, at least among security organizations, that she's missing. The fact does not appear on public news services."

"It wouldn't," said Paul. "Most Corporatia families are very tight-lipped regarding their personal lives."

"You being an exception."

"Only with you, Yoelin," Paul amended, and sipped his coffee. "Only with you."

"This makes a trip to Tiratanga all the more imperative," said Yoelin. She got up. "We don't want to miss the concert, Paul."

*

Naked and sweating, Yoelin and Paul stood behind the hologram that sealed off their Cave and waited for the evening winds to begin. The night air failed to chill either of them, yet Yoelin still felt a little *frisson* scuttle up her spine. It was not possible for her to forget the hour that had just passed—an hour she had not dared hope would come for her. Emotionally if not physically she was monogamous; Paul Wroclawski was the only man for whom she would drop everything and come running if he called. And he could never call.

Still, at least he was here. She found herself wondering what that meant. Never before had she involved him in her Rescues, yet he had leaped to her rescue as if he had been waiting by his Palmetto for her to call. His personal life had not changed; he was still married. Now he had a son. Two years, Paul had said. But much could happen—so much could *change*, in two years.

And she would drop *almost* everything, except her Rescue work. That was her self-identity. She was unable to envision herself doing anything else, even—ye gods!—married to Paul. Would he accept that of her? She had never asked him; the prospect of what he might say, terrified her.

"The wind is picking up," said Paul.

Still fighting off insecurities, she barely heard him. He remained a mystery to her. He had said, in effect, that he would give up his life to be with her. That was more than she could give him. But the

Wroclawski family had dominated Resources for the last three centuries, ever since the inception of Corporatia. She could not allow him to give up his position, if for no other reason than that the corporations needed people like him to balance those hierarchs who had few scruples. Like herself, he was doing some good where he was.

She hissed something, and he turned to look at her.

"You're upset," he said, his tone inviting her to explain.

She shook her head. "Not now, Paul. Please."

He turned back to the hologram. The wind was indeed blowing, and already in the distance, as it brushed past the first few of the twenty-four Cave openings, she could detect the hoarse whispered sounds of a *shakuhachi* flute. The idea was to create a tune by opening and closing various Cave holograms, in the same fashion that a flute might be played. When the direction of the wind was just right, the melody became plaintive and haunting . . .

It began.

A hologram or two opened and closed, changing the tune that had begun—a simple tune that set the mood. Yoelin slipped an arm around Paul and leaned against him. A Cave opened and remained open, while others further down the line from them fluttered. Yoelin, who had hoped for a romantic tune, found this one depressing. Perhaps it was the fluttering in the distance. Someone there had experience with the Cave winds. Was the flautist depressed, too? The image that came to her was that of a lost soul, pining for a life that was slowly being sucked from . . . her.

She began to weep.

Unable to perform her beloved and vital Rescues. Unable to have for more than a night the one man she loved. Unable to remain in one place for too long, lest she be identified and located, and captured by Clewthe's gang. Unable even to open the Cave to contribute to the melody, for fear of being spotted.

Paul opened the Cave. Yoelin screamed. A man was standing five or six paces away, head keened as if listening to the music. He turned at the sound of her scream, surprise and puzzlement crossing his face.

"*Close it*," Yoelin cried.

Paul did so immediately. "What is it?" he asked. "What's wrong?"

She could not find her voice.

"Is it that man?" he pressed.

"Yes . . . no! Oh, I don't know." She turned away from him, and tottered toward the bed to sit down on the edge of it. Hands folded in her lap, she stared down at the thick maroon carpet between her bare feet and despised herself for her moment of weakness. Yet only with Paul might she let herself go. Was her inner strength then a mere façade to protect her weakness from others?

The bed sank a little; Paul had sat down nearby. Yoelin did not look at him. She hoped he had the intuition not to try to touch her. She had to fight through this on her own. Slowly she began to rock her upper body, forward and back, in a rhythm to music she could only imagine. In the vague distance, she could hear the wistful *shakuhachi* as if it were calling to her.

The bed lightened; Paul had gotten up. She sensed, rather than saw, him crossing the room to acquire some object. Presently he stood before her, a pastel blue bathrobe draped over his arm. He held it out to her. After a moment, she stood up, accepted it from him, and slung it around her body, tying the belt in front, in a simple bow. A tiny nod of gratitude was all she was strong enough to give him.

He said no words to her, but garbed himself in a matching robe before seating himself in the chair by the writing table. He seemed to have the patience of a clock. He was waiting for her, for whenever she had need of him, in whatever way she might need him.

Yoelin sat down and leaned back, supported by stiff arms. No longer did she hang her head. She spoke as if the weight of her burden had shifted, lightened. She could see more clearly now.

"Clewthe is the head of a very powerful gang," she told him. "You knew I was sold and shipped out as a child, to pay off my father's gambling debts." He nodded, and she continued, "The debts were owed to Clewthe's gang. He agreed to take me in exchange—but murdered my parents anyway. But I never arrived; I escaped that fate, only to be dealt that of an adolescent courtesan, as you know. I have no doubt he is still looking for me, even after a quarter of a century."

Paul found a low voice, and used it gently. "It's why you keep moving around," he said. "And why you changed your name."

"Yes."

"Yoelin, I can protect you."

She shook her head. "He is insidious. He reaches anywhere he wants."

"Yoelin—"

"Don't you think I researched him?" she argued. "Don't you think he would be the one person I would deliberately kill, if I could get to him? If he ever finds out I'm really Deirdre Hanratty, he'll—"

"Maybe he has."

Aghast, she stared at him. "What?"

"The man who accosted you at the kiosk," Paul reminded her. "Could he have been sent by Clewthe?"

Briefly she considered this, and shook her head again. "No, I don't think so. He wanted me alive if possible, dead otherwise. Clewthe would want me alive. He would not kill me until his use of me balanced the debt he was owed, plus interest. It's more likely that man was from something else."

"I'm sorry," said Paul. "I know this is painful, but I have to ask: could he have been killing off your clients?"

She winced; he was right, the reminder made her ache all over. "It's possible," she said, against the doubt in her tone. "But to what end, Paul?"

He smiled. "Thus, your council of war."

"Thank you. Paul?"

"Right here."

"We'll leave for Tiratanga in the morning. Tonight . . . I need to be held."

"I can do that."

009

Downdock on Tiratanga proved more complicated than Yoelin had anticipated, and she was glad of Paul's company in yet another way. His identification and voice command got the *Sequana* through the network of security satellites and onto the tarmac of the Tiratanga Port Authority Spaceport. He also arranged private parking for the 'skiff once he and Yoelin had been cleared. He did not identify her by name, only as Plus 1; his name alone warded off personal questions.

"Stiff," said Yoelin, referring to the entry procedures, as they emerged through the hatch and into the bright light of yellow-white Alcoda.

For the arrival she had chosen an ultra-feminine outfit consisting of an ankle-length floral print skirt that sculpted her legs when she walked, and a pale blue pullover blouse loose enough to conceal her weaponry and cut to entice if she should lean forward a little. Distraction was the name of her game at the moment—she concealed her abilities behind her appearance as a "Plus 1".

"You'll pass through a weapons scanner at Port Authority," he reminded her, as they passed along a security tunnel that led to Port Entry. He flashed a grin, adding, "If you get caught, I don't know you." Then, soberly: "And I don't see how you can not get caught."

"Professional secret."

They walked slowly in the sunlight; a few other arrivals squeezed past them, murmuring apologies, while others remained bottlenecked behind them. Paul walked with the air of a top hierarch, which he was; his blue and brown leisure suit cost thalers in four figures. Although not prone to ostentation, he had selected his attire and demeanor to impress the Thibbony family—which in any case would already be impressed by his pedigree.

The arrivals bunched together in a single-file line to pass through the weapons detectors. Yoelin sensed Paul holding his breath as they fit through without incident. The expression on his face afterwards brought a smile to her lips.

"I don't believe it," he said. "How did you do that?"

"Told you."

Now they were out in the open. Ground shuttles awaited the arrivals, to take them to the main Terminal, where they would sort out their destinations. The low skyline beyond the Terminal impressed Yoelin, who had seen others, but not like this. Where the buildings of other cities of Corporatia ascended as if to touch the stars, those in Tiratanga City sprawled casually across the landscape. She already knew that powered pathways connected most of the structures, so that businessfolk and clients and visitors need only step aboard and relax until they reached their destinations. However, Paul assured her of a quicker and smoother approach.

"We can stop in one of the Terminal cafés, if you like," he suggested, as they boarded a shuttle and sat down side by side.

"I'm not overwhelmed," she told him. "But it never hurts to get one's bearings, if the opportunity arises."

"More professional secrets?"

"Common sense." She gave him a sidelong glance. "Can you really raise Aramis Thibbony on your Palmetto?"

Paul clucked at her. "Only now you think to ask me?"

"I trust you."

"Aramis and my father are on close terms," he said. "After all, exploited resources require transportation to processing centers."

A breeze came up, cooling them. Yoelin found herself missing trees. Surely there were some on Tiratanga, but none for as far as she could see. Development had uprooted forests to make way for commerce. She did not regard it as a fair trade, but Tiratanga City was located in the planet's temperate zone. Much further south, and the costs of air conditioning might prove prohibitive. As it was, she felt a thin sheen of perspiration build up on her forehead; she wished she had brought a hat.

"Please tell me how you managed to pass through the detector," said Paul, his voice lowered for privacy.

She leaned closer to him—not that she needed any motivation—and whispered, "Detectors are set to scan for plastic weaponry with energy packets, and non-energy plastic weapons," she explained. "I'm carrying a five-hundred-year-old steel pistol—I believe the designation back then was an M1911A1 forty-five caliber automatic pistol—used for close combat in the military. It wouldn't show up, and neither would the Kolal knife."

She leaned back, and continued, "Paul, I'm not going to be caught without a sidearm again. If I can get through the detectors, it's a good bet the opposition will figure a way to do the same."

They reached the Terminal. Inside the great open bay, vast tinted windows controlled the sunlight. Cooler air circulated, carrying with it the aromas of food and beverages, the faint scents of expensive perfumes and colognes, and just a dash of hot cooking oil. Her hunger goaded, Yoelin looked around for a likely place to sit down in private over an iced tea and listen while Paul made contact with the most important man on the planet.

There were kiosks and shops abound. At first the bustling commercial traffic made little sense to Yoelin, who had reckoned Tiratanga to be a center for records and transportation arrangements and bills of lading. What she now saw, especially in the shop windows, altered that viewpoint. Goods from all over the Spiral Arm were brought here, some at great expense, to attract everyone from the wealthy down to the meanest scullery personnel. Tiratanga—at least the City—was an interstellar entrepôt. She supposed that some of the people she saw shopping had come from other worlds to do so. That did not bode well for her; it meant that whoever was watching her might already be on Tiratanga, possibly as one of the shoppers.

Still, the Terminal was not crowded; Yoelin estimated that some two hundred people were browsing here and there. Several individuals caught her attention, by the way they walked, or carried themselves, or studiously looked straight ahead and not at her. Finally she shrugged. A little paranoia never hurt in her line of work. But she did not yet get the sense that anyone was watching for her.

"There," said Paul, startling her from her dark thoughts.

Yoelin looked where he pointed, and saw an outdoor café with a small deli, and empty of patrons for the moment. Round white tables with frame-and-mesh chairs, in no discernible pattern, stood in front, and a black man in cook's whites stood awaiting custom.

Now Paul was pointing to a particular table. "If we sit there," he said, "you'll be able to watch the approaches."

Yoelin, who had already chosen that table for that reason, merely smiled. As they approached, the food clerk smiled, and waved them to the table they had obviously selected. "*Karibu chakula*," he said. On his apron he wore a name tag that identified him as Hamisi.

Paul held the chair for her, and she sat down. Ignoring the laminated menu on the table, she gazed up at the food clerk. "*Tafadhali, tuletee kahawa na mkate na siagi*," she told him politely.

Hamisi beamed at her.

Paul's jaw dropped. His question projected quiet astonishment. "You speak . . . whatever that is, too?"

"It's Swahili," said Yoelin. "He invited us to come and eat, so I asked him for coffee, bread, and butter."

"*Unataka nyama, matunda?*" offered Hamisi.

Yoelin shook her head, and he hustled off. Paul's lips puffed out as he blew a sigh. "You never cease to amaze me."

"I have a varied clientele," she explained, and saddened. "Had," she amended.

"And will have again," he told her. "Do you think he speaks Standard?" he asked.

"Probably better than we do," she replied. "The Swahili is for atmosphere. He didn't expect a response in it. But we can talk here. Hamisi would not think to betray our confidences now."

"Different worlds, you and I," said Paul.

Yoelin felt a tear begin to well, and fought it off. Paul was right: they came from two different worlds, and no matter what he gave up in order to be with her, he would still strive to lift her. She had her place, had established her place, even if her life was itinerant. She was—had been—doing some good, and would do more once she had resolved the present crisis. She had known all this in her heart; Paul's words now brought the conflict out into the open. He loved her, of that she had no doubt; he would do anything for her. She loved him; she would do *almost* anything for him. Almost. And that difference between them was deadly. She could not—would not—be other than who she was. And neither, in the end result, could he.

The coffee arrived—Harrar from Ethiopia, Hamisi said—and a bowl of warm rolls and a plate of pats of soft butter. They sipped and ate in silence. Unable for the moment to look at Paul, Yoelin watched the passers-by without really seeing them. People appeared to her in swatches of color, like an Impressionist's landscape. She gazed through them. Finally, Paul's voice penetrated her consciousness.

"What was that?" she asked.

"I think I've upset you," he said again. "But I don't know what I did."

"You didn't do anything, Paul," she said, her voice soft and low—not her bedroom voice, but one reserved for responses to questions she was not yet ready to answer. She was about to add a bit of reassurance when a man walked past their table, and she froze. His bare left arm sported a tattoo like that on the man who had tried to take her prisoner in the kiosk on Prana.

010

Yoelin held her breath. The man passed on, apparently without noticing her. He seemed to be perusing the kiosks and shops along her side of the bay. He did not glance over his shoulder, but he did stop at a display window. She thought he might have had an angle there in which to see her reflection, but she could not be certain. Still, it was a professional maneuver for him to make. But what was his profession?

She dared not follow him. But Paul could.

"Yoelin?" he said, before she could speak. His eyes were darker, his brow knit in concern.

"Twenty meters to our left," she said quietly, urgently. "No, don't look! He's in front of the display window. Dark hair, medium length, about your height, blue short-sleeved work shirt, brown trousers, sturdy dark sprayshoe."

"Got him."

Yoelin's heart warmed: no questions.

"If he turns away from us," she continued, "get up and move out to the center of the bay. Act casual, but watch where he goes. If he stops, try to blend in with others . . . okay, there he goes."

Paul got to his feet, waved at Hamisi, and followed her instructions. He merged so well with other shoppers and travelers that she almost lost sight of him. Realization set in, sobering her. This was not his sort of business. She doubted anyone would take action against him here, but it was not beyond the realm of possibility.

It was also possible that the tattoo was coincidence—not that she believed that for a second—or that the man killed by Velanne Moths on Prana was acting on his own volition, for reasons not yet clear.

She could not see Paul. Neither could she see the man he was tracking.

Panic quickened her heart. She had made a mistake, sending him out. He had no business in her business. *Where had Paul gotten to?*

She half-rose, and sat back down. That might not be the only person with that tattoo lurking about, perhaps watching for her. A blue octopus was not all that uncommon. That both of the two she had seen had been inked onto the outside of the left forearm increased the probability of a relationship.

She paused to consider. An octopus—eight legs, each of which bore suckers for grabbing and holding onto. The analogy meant something to someone.

Had the octopus grabbed Paul?

Where are you? she cried silently. She cursed herself for having sent him.

"More bread?" asked Hamisi.

Yoelin's heart made a lump in her throat as she started to reach under her blouse for the pistol.

Hamisi took a step back. "I did not mean to startle you," he apologized.

She swallowed hard, and returned her attention to the Terminal bay, searching. "I was expecting someone else," she told him.

"Your friend? Perhaps he has gone to buy you a gift."

She smiled, though he could not see it. "Perhaps. Do you see where he has gone?"

He made a little gesture toward the other side of the bay. "He is making a purchase from that jewelry kiosk," he said.

Yoelin sighed, exasperated. *Of course* Hamisi could see Paul, for he was standing while she, sitting, had a lower angle of vision. "Is he okay?" she asked.

"Yes. Why should he not be? You will let me know if you want anything else?" he added quickly, in Swahili, and hurried off.

"*Asante,*" she thanked his back, and focused all her attention on Paul, returning.

On the way across the bay, he had eyes only for her. No sideways glance gave her a clue as to the location of the man with the tattoo; he might be anywhere. Meanwhile, a new patron arrived—well-dressed and of sturdy build. A glance up at his face as he swept past her table left her with a quick view of a squarish head haired and bearded in dusty brown. She gave scant thought to him—probably he was going to order something from the deli—until protests from Hamisi reached her ears.

Yoelin listened carefully. Very little of what Hamisi said was intelligible to her. A few phrases snuck through, a mix of Standard and Swahili that surprised her, for she knew he was adept in both languages and had no need of polyglot. His voice seemed to be pitched higher than she recalled. She resisted the urge to turn around, as Hamisi did not sound as if he were in any physical danger. Only at the risk of revealing her skills might she intervene. Still, if Hamisi were to be harmed . . .

You just can't close down the Rescues, she thought.

The argument—for that's what it was—ended; the man left. As he did so, he passed by Yoelin's table once more, and this time she caught a glimpse of his left arm. It bore the tattoo of a blue octopus.

Paul quickened his approach; evidently her face had revealed an emotion of which she was unaware. He yanked, rather than pulled out, his chair and sat down to face her. Hard pale eyes examined her. "Are you all right?" he asked. "What's wrong?"

Yoelin threw a glance over her shoulder at Hamisi. Despite the dour expression on his face, he appeared to be in no danger. Paul's hand on her arm returned her attention to him.

"I'm just trying to make sense of all this," she told him, and took a sip of coffee. It had already cooled. In a few words, she explained to him what had just transpired.

Listening, Paul cast several glances in Hamisi's direction. "He seems to be calm enough now," said Paul, when she had finished. He hesitated. "Yoelin, are you looking for someone to Rescue?"

She felt her eyes flash briefly, but her voice was even and cool when she responded. "As a sort of compensation? No, Paul, I know what I heard, even if I didn't grasp the full context." She paused for a moment. "What did you learn?" she asked him.

He made a face. "Not much. He stopped at several shops, remonstrated with two or three shopkeepers, and generally moved on down the line. I lost track of him at the far exit. He had no apparent interest in you. Barking at shadows, Yoelin?"

Now she sat back, angry. "Are you doubting me, Paul?"

"No, no, I—"

"Because I know there's something going on here," she said tersely.

"I just can't see what it is. Yet."

She started to add that this was her kind of business and that she knew what she was doing in it—but she had already told him as much, more than once. It was time she reminded herself of that as well. She got up and stepped toward the deli bar, where Hamisi was slicing smoked meat. He glanced up from the cutting board as she drew near.

"Hamisi, *habari mchana gani?*" she asked him. What is that all about?

He kept to Swahili. "It is nothing, *bibi.* Do not trouble yourself."

His undercoat of fear shone through to her like a beacon. "Truly I wish to know, Hamisi," she soothed. "Are we not friends?"

For several seconds he gave her a hard look that she was unable to read. Finally he laid down the butcher knife and stood staring down at the meat he had cut.

"Hamisi?" she said quietly.

He lifted his eyes to hers; they were wet. "My great-grandfather was brought out into space as a slave from Nairobi," he told her. "He labored on several worlds, fathered several children, and managed to secure safety for two of them, including my grandfather, who was free. From his father he learned his trade," his hand made a little motion over the meat, "which he passed through my father to me, as you see."

"But you are an educated man, Hamisi," she pointed out.

He nodded once. "I attended the Marney Gardner college of History at the University of Tiratanga, graduating after several years. I had to support myself and my family, you see, so I was not always able to take a useful course when it was offered."

Yoelin raised a hand, stopping him. "Perhaps we should move to Standard," she said, with a light chuckle. "My Swahili is not that good. *Nafahamu kidogo ki-swahili.*"

Now he flashed his first smile. "But of course."

"So, you graduated," she cued.

"Oh, yes. Full marks, for the most part. I have an application filed with the Historical Institute." His expression fell. "Not that there's much hope of getting in there. I was thinking about saving up enough money for us to ship out to The Dragons and settle. But circumstances make that difficult."

"How so?"

Hamisi glanced left and right. "I'd . . . best not say."

"It has something to do with that man who was here," said Yoelin. It was not a question.

Hamisi sighed, deflated.

"I could not help but overhear some of it," she went on. "The way you spoke was . . . , well, it was not you. Not who I think is you."

He raised a hand, a plea for her to stop. "It is trouble for you, *bibi*," he told her. "It is what I live with."

"How much do you give him?" she asked. "And how often?"

Hamisi hung his head and muttered something in Swahili beyond her working vocabulary. His fingertips stroked the butcher knife as if it were his child. Finally, he picked it up and scraped the sliced meat into a stainless-steel bin for customers to select. Then he turned away.

"Hamisi," Yoelin said quietly.

He remained standing with his back to her. His shoulders slumped, and he shook his head—at himself, not at her. His voice was barely audible when he spoke. "We do not talk about it," he said.

"Perhaps it is time to talk about it," countered Yoelin.

He turned around, his expression one of defeat. "What can you do?"

"I won't know that, until I know what the problem is."

He stepped closer to the deli bar.

"What you tell me, I did not hear from you," she promised him.

Hamisi drew a deep breath. "I will answer. Fifty thalers every five days. I lease this kiosk. Fifty thalers represents a quarter of my profits."

"I didn't hear a thing," said Yoelin. "It must be the air circulator. Who is that man, Hamisi? Who is he?"

"They bear the sign of the blue octopus," he replied, and looked as if he wanted to spit somewhere. "The sign of the gang of Clewthe."

011

The revelation left Yoelin speechless. Dimly she was aware that Hamisi had begun to watch her closely, a question in his dark eyes. She was remembering a tattoo on a man who had shot at her before being killed himself. Who had wanted her alive if possible, dead if that was the only way. A man from Clewthe.

Clewthe had found her, after all these years.

She wanted to cry.

Ye gods . . .

A hand at her side, an arm around her. She knew without seeing that Paul had spotted something he did not like, and had come to her aid. Another hand on her other arm, this one dark brown: Hamisi was assisting her to the chair at the table. The two men seated her. Hamisi muttered something about a drink; she doubted it would be water.

They had found her . . .

She heard her name, and turned toward the sound of it. Paul had turned his chair to face her. They were sitting with their knees almost touching, with her hands in his. Although her eyes were dry, she did not see him clearly. He seemed distant, a relic from her past brought forward to her without the passing of time.

She felt as if her world had just come to an end . . .

"What is it?" she heard.

Her lungs demanded air; she had stopped breathing. Phlegm in her throat whistled as she gulped a series of quick but shallow breaths. The bay spun around her. She clutched Paul's hands for balance, but felt her eyes strain as they started to scroll up.

She heard her name.

A clear crystal mug of some dark liquid appeared before her on the table as if by magic. A chair squeaked as it was being pulled toward the table. Hamisi sat down on it, close enough for comfort, not so close as to intrude. Yoelin reached for the mug, grasped it, lifted it to her lips. The liquid in it smelled faintly of molasses and tasted of a very potent rum. She took two swallows and set the mug back down. The world around her gradually came back into focus.

Yoelin drew her hands from Paul's and sat up straight. The dizziness had passed, to be replaced by a clarity of vision but not yet of purpose.

"I'm all right," she said. But her voice shook. She cleared her throat, and continued. "Paul, it's Clewthe. The blue octopus tattoo identifies his people. The man on Prana was after me. They've found me, Paul. And I don't see any options."

"You know this Clewthe?" asked Hamisi.

She turned to him. "From my past. He was . . ." She paused, reflecting. Enough was enough. Hamisi was in the present; so should she be. "I have a past, Hamisi," she told him. "It's over, even if there are ghosts. This is me, here and now."

"I understand."

Yoelin believed him. He was like her: he'd had to pull himself up, by dint of hard labor and hard study. Some of his journey remained to him, as did some of hers. He knew whereof she had spoken; in his own way, he had been there.

Gently she touched the back of Paul's hand. "It's all right," she said. "This is my kind of business. Something will come to mind. In the meantime—"

"What does that mean?" Hamisi broke in. He sat back, frowning and defensive. "What is this 'business' you speak of?"

She tried to disarm him with a smile. "It's nothing illegal," she assured him. "At least, most of the time it's not. It's just that sometimes I . . . help people. Children, especially. Please let's just leave it at that."

"As you wish," Hamisi said, in a dead monotone. He got up and returned to the deli bar.

Paul kept his voice confidentially low. "He thinks you're part of a gang, too," he said.

"I know. Rival gangs fighting over the same turf."

"You should tell him."

She gaped at him. "And tell him what?" she snapped, her tone rising with budding anger. "That I'm the Guardian Angel? Paul, if I don't resolve this, I dare not reopen my Rescue sites. Do you understand what that means? What it means to me? It means I can't be me, anymore."

"You can be someone else, then," he temporized. "Yoelin, this is not the end of the world."

"Not the end of *your* world," she shot back. "You can always buy a recovery, if you have to. I can't."

"Is that what's bothering—"

"I'm sorry, Paul," she broke in quickly. "I shouldn't have said that."

But it had been said, and now her heart ached, for him and for herself.

Paul's teeth worried at his lower lip. Finally he said, "It's time for me to contact the Thibbony Family and arrange a meeting."

"Yes," Yoelin said dully. "You should do that."

*

Paul was unable to raise Aramis Thibbony directly. The communications center at Corporatia Transportation connected him with one office after another, the first five of which had no idea where to direct him. On the sixth attempt, he hit pay dirt: the respondent secretary passed him to Aramis's personal majordomo, one Tomas Delgado, whose half-meter hologram stood before Paul on the table, next to the basket of rolls.

"Paul Wroclawski," said Delgado. His hologram showed a thin man with a light build, who held himself as if he worked out twice a day, possibly at soccer or tennis. His dark hair was shorn to within a couple millimeters of his scalp. With his range of vision restricted to Paul's image, Delgado's black eyes did not bother with the peripheral views, where Yoelin held back, watching his face for reactions. "I believe we met, some years ago," Delgado went on. He spoke with a clipped accent and broad vowels. "I've heard about your father. My condolences."

"Thank you," said Paul. "I know you're busy, so I'll get right to the point. You've hired out a locator to find a woman named Yoelin Thibbony."

Delgado inclined his head. "That task has been assigned to Velanne Moths, after some . . . difficulties. If I might ask, Paul, how are you interested?"

"You wanted her found. I've found her. She's with me."

82

The news seemed to startle Delgado, who frowned, obviously trying to figure out an angle, while Paul blandly sipped at his coffee.

At last Delgado asked, "What is it you want?"

Paul shrugged. "I want to deliver her to Aramis, and collect the finder's fee, from you, I would guess."

Delgado issued a dry chuckle. "I was not aware of your financial difficulties."

"A thaler saved is a thaler earned."

"Quite. Where are you?" Paul told him, and Delgado said, "I'll send a car round for you. Fifteen minutes."

"Thank you," said Paul, as the hologram faded.

After it had gone completely, Yoelin said, "I don't like it."

"He didn't even ask to see you," mused Paul. He rubbed his chin as if a beard were there. "You may be right," he went on. "Games within games." He paused, and said softly, "Yoelin—"

She shook her head vehemently, and buttered and ate two bread rolls in silence.

By the time she had finished the second one, a stocky man in a neat tan uniform approached them. His right hand clutched a driving cap. His left upper sleeve bore the patch of Corporatia Transportation, with the brown winged wheel on a beige field. He came to a halt two paces away and introduced himself with a stiff bow as Skandor Hegyes, sent by Tomas Delgado to deliver them to Headquarters. Yoelin studied him unobtrusively and concluded that he was unarmed. Hegyes, on the other hand, scarcely seemed to notice her.

Paul stood up and said, "Lead the way."

The car turned out to be a tan airfoil adorned on either side with the Transportation emblem. It was docked outside a side door of the Terminal like an after-thought. One passenger, a man also attired in uniform, sat in the front seat, watching the open doorway from which they emerged. He snapped to, got out, and held the airfoil's side gate for Paul and Yoelin to climb into the back seat. Hegyes hatted himself and fastened the chinstrap, then powered up the conveyance and pulled away smoothly—professionally, noted Yoelin.

She sat back, eyes narrowed, thinking. Hegyes had performed exactly as he should have done, were he a professional chauffeur in the employ of a vast corporation. Neat and precise, he operated the airfoil as if he had been doing so all his life. He was holding the craft at two meters above the glideway, at a steady rate of thirty kilometers per hour. She gave a sidelong glance at Paul; he seemed relaxed. The passing breeze ruffled his hair, as it did hers. She grew watchful of the passenger, who had not been introduced. He was—should have been—superfluous. This was a simple driving task; if a problem arose, Hegyes could summon assistance. So why had the man been brought along?

For one terrible moment, Yoelin found herself wondering whether Paul was in on it, on whatever was about to transpire. He had, after all, separated himself from her while following the tattooed man. He could have communicated with Delgado earlier. Could have—but what would be the point?

They came upon a Y intersection, with both glideways bypassing a vast, fenced garden of trees, shrubs, and flowers. Yoelin detected the faintest whiff of lilacs brought to her on the oncoming breeze. The glideway on the right led out toward a forest and some hilly terrain; that on the left passed along the bend of a river and then back toward the corporate compound.

Hegyes took the right glideway. Yoelin nodded to herself; so be it.

"Scenic route?" she called toward the front.

"We have a few minutes before *M'sieur* Delgado can see you," Hegyes explained. "A previously scheduled meeting. We thought you might enjoy a look around."

Yoelin smiled at the rear-view mirror, and nodded politely. The response made perfect sense. Just like Hegyes' comportment and driving abilities. Everything fit. Everything, except the passenger.

"It's not much further," Hegyes called back.

"What's that?" asked Paul.

The passenger turned abruptly, pointing a Krupp Stern in their general direction.

012

Yoelin gathered herself. "I'd like an explanation," she said.

"On the other side of the forest is a ravine," said Hegyes. "You two got out to look at the view, and she slipped and fell. Very sad. This is what you will tell Corporatia Security, *M'sieur* Wroclawski, should they inquire. You will then depart from Tiratanga and return to Lowella to await the death of your father."

Yoelin licked her lips, faking the expression of fear. "Why are you doing this?" she wanted to know.

Hegyes shrugged. "Orders."

"From?" asked Paul.

The question startled Yoelin. If Paul were in on the conspiracy to kill her, he would not have asked. Even so, it did not dispel all her doubts about him.

"Well?" she said. "Do I at least get to know who wants me dead?"

The passenger held his energy sidearm casually, now that he had established control with it. "Delgado, of course," he replied.

"Of course," said Yoelin.

In one deft move she tugged the pistol free and shot the passenger through the back of his seat. He died with his eyes wide open in shock.

The reports made Hegyes jerk his hand at the controls, but he managed to keep the airfoil righted. "You," he sputtered, "you were . . . we were told you were unarmed."

"Oh, dear," she replied. "Were you?"

The unsolicited statement confirmed Paul's innocence to Yoelin. Knowing she was carrying, had he been involved, he would have passed on that bit of information.

"Dock it down," Paul demanded.

Hegyes complied. "What are you going to do?" he asked.

Paul looked to Yoelin for the answer. "No choice," she said, and fired two rounds into Hegyes' back.

"Yoelin!" gasped Paul.

She climbed forward. "Help me get them out of their seats," she ordered.

"What are you going to do?"

Not "we," she noted.

"What they were going to do," she told him, as they tugged Hegyes' body aft. "Drop them off at the ravine. Then we'll see how Delgado receives us when you deliver me to him."

The passenger's body was next. "Next I suppose you'll remind me that this is your kind of business," Paul complained. "This . . . killing, this cold disposal."

She straightened, and transfixed him with a look that was violent in its lack of expression. He recoiled. With calm ferocity she said, "Yes, it's my kind of business. I don't like killing, Paul. You of all people should know that. But I won't risk my life or yours by leaving alive someone who would if possible get one or both of us killed. Those are the rules, Paul."

"It's just that I've never seen this side of you."

She climbed onto the pilot's seat. "I don't show it often," she said, as she powered up and took off.

They rounded the forest in silence, and Yoelin found herself worrying about what Paul was thinking. "Different worlds," he had pointed out. Now she was showing him first-hand just how different. Yet Paul himself possessed the power and authority to order the death of someone. She wondered whether he had ever exercised it. But it was not a question she would ever ask him.

Instead, she steeled herself to what had to be done.

Soon they came upon the promised ravine. She brought the airfoil to hover above it, and together—Paul obviously reluctant—they pitched the bodies overboard, to plummet a couple hundred meters into the bottom of the ravine.

"Shouldn't we at least say a few words?" Paul asked her.

The airfoil continued to hover at her command. "I'd only tell them that I was glad it was them and not us."

Paul exploded. "Damn it, Yoelin, that's not what I meant! Ye gods, must you be so cavalier about it?"

"You're the one who recommended me long ago to Corporatia Security," she pointed out, with some asperity. "What do you think I did for them, make coffee?" A pained expression came over her; she had gone too far. She temporized, trying to restore order, trying to reweave the fraying edges of their relationship. "Delgado wanted me dead, Paul. Those two men were his agents. They'd've killed you, too, if you gave them any sign at all that you were unwilling to cooperate with the scheme. Aren't you the least bit curious as to why they were willing to risk an intercorporate war by killing a potential corporate chair?"

Breath left Paul. His mouth worked, and finally he found a response. "I hadn't thought of that," he mumbled.

Yoelin powered the airfoil away, returning the way they had come in order to take the other prong of the Y intersection.

"Can you raise Aramis Thibbony directly, without going through Delgado?" she asked.

"I believe so," he answered. "But what if Aramis ordered this?"

She dodged the airfoil around a copse of white-barked trees. "Then I will be very surprised," she said.

"Are you thinking this is a palace coup?" he asked, as he keyed his Palmetto.

She hesitated. "I'm . . . not sure. But history is full of instances where the grand vizier, or majordomo, or cardinal, or executive secretary, was the real power on the throne. What I can't figure out is where I fit into all this." She paused, with a glance in his direction. "Who are you raising?"

"My father," he answered, readily enough. "I'll ask him to talk with Aramis, and have him meet us in Delgado's office . . . yes, hello, Dad? I have a bit of an urgent problem here . . ."

The communication was one-sided, but Yoelin heard enough to know that Paul was doing exactly as he told her. Still, she was unable to shunt away entirely her earlier suspicion of Paul. Little nagging doubts, more so than infidelity or addiction, made a troubled relationship more difficult to resolve. In the latter instances, the solution was obvious: leave. But what if . . .

And what would be the point of Paul's hypothetical betrayal? As far as she knew, he stood to gain nothing by it. Quite the contrary, and by his own admission, he was better off with her safe.

They reached the Y intersection. "And?" pressed Yoelin.

"He'll do it, of course," Paul answered. "He and Aramis go way back. Yoelin?"

Uh-oh, she thought. "Yes?"

"You seem uneasy."

I don't want to talk about it right now. "Let's just get this over with," she said tersely.

They skirted a large pond, an artificial estuary of the river, where a pair of black swans swam. An elegant gazebo stood at the narrow end of the pond, and a pier extended from it out into the water. An old man sat there, fishing. Yoelin cocked an eyebrow at Paul, who shrugged.

"Former staff enjoying the fruits of retirement," was his assessment.

Ahead loomed the corporate compound. On either wing stood low office buildings of structural plastic, pale green with dark green trim, dedicated to the mechanics of transportation arrangements. The centerpiece, an estate house of fitted stone and ornate wood and fronted by a long colonnade of white plastic that led up to the door, dominated the view. Its architecture clashed with the two wings, but no one would complain and risk offending all that wealth. Yoelin found herself wishing she knew a little more about the family, but the details she sought were well-protected, and would take a determined—and illegal—effort to uncover.

The estate gardens, where Morrainee Thibbony had last been seen, spread to the east, to the left of the colonnade. The shrubbery was dense enough for concealment. If someone meant to abduct the young woman, all he had to do was wait until she took her regular walk through the flowers. If she intended to flee from the estate, she might have concealed a conveyance somewhere within the garden. No one would notice, either way, until it was too late.

But Ellis Darden believed Morrainee had been abducted.

West of the colonnade, several airfoils were parked. Yoelin docked down there, and they disembarked. Her heart beat a little faster now; she did not know what to expect as they climbed the few steps to the double oak doors.

"No buttons, no knockers," said Paul.

Yoelin made a little gesture. "Try the bell pull."

"Oh. How quaint."

A gong sounded inside. A moment later, the right door was pulled open by a portly and balding middle-aged man garbed in what Yoelin thought of as butler black. A black bow tie secured the collar of his ruffled white shirt. He had thick, soft hands whose fingers had undergone many manicures. His pale gray eyes widened just a little when he looked at Yoelin, but he addressed Paul.

"Come in, please," he said. "You are expected."

Yoelin and Paul followed him inside, and across a receiving room that gave her a cavernous yawn. A floor of dark hardwood reflected light like a mirror, and she was able to watch each footfall as it struck. But looking down at her mobile reflection was slightly dizzying; she turned her attention to the walls.

There hung several oil paintings in thick, ornate frames. Yoelin recognized a couple of them, and suspected that the names of the other artists would prove familiar. One painting, of a medieval seaport on Earth, was almost certainly a Tintoretto.

"Ye gods," she whispered.

Light blue plastic walls had been textured to an unobtrusive matte, to accentuate the art. She made her way past wide cylindrical plinths of marble that supported delicate vases with intricate designs, and gold and jade artifacts from ancient Earth civilizations. Before the central staircase that led to the private rooms on the second level, a marble fountain burbled over statues of aquatic goddesses and mermaids, the design reminding Yoelin of a Bernini fountain. She wondered whether the Thibbony Family had arranged to have it brought from Rome.

They wound around the staircase and came to a heavy hardwood door. The butler knocked three times on it, and they heard a command to enter. As the butler opened the door, Yoelin's hand dipped toward the butt of the automatic pistol.

Inside, behind a teakwood desk, stood the man whose hologram had graced their table in the Terminal: Tomas Delgado. He looked none too happy. Yoelin's eyes went to the elderly man standing beside the desk. Paul's wave of greeting to him told her that this was Aramis Thibbony. She felt his gaze descend upon her like soft light. His smile was wide enough to include the canines.

"Morrainee!" he exclaimed. "But—what have you done to your hair? You know I like it red." Arms wide, he moved forward. "Come give your old dad a hug," he pleaded. "What have you been up to since breakfast? Another walk in the garden?"

Ye, thought Yoelin, *gods*.

013

Anxiety percolated in Yoelin's stomach as she struggled to assess this development, playing along as she accepted Thibbony's embrace of greeting. He smelled of expensive body lotion and hints of after-shave and good whiskey. He kissed her on each cheek; his skin felt smooth and soft. She peered over his shoulder at Delgado. The executive secretary was shifting his weight from one leg to the other and back, as if he were debating whether to flee or to take precipitate action. His narrowed eyes watched her carefully. Yoelin tightened her grip on the butt of the pistol, her thumb poised to flip off the safety as she drew it. If she had to draw it.

Thibbony held her back at arm's length. "You mustn't neglect your studies, my dear," he asked her. "I called the university, and they said you weren't in class today."

"I'm sorry," said Yoelin, contrite. "I didn't mean to worry you."

Thibbony shook his head. "It's all right now," he said, as he led her toward a side door. "It's all right."

Yoelin resisted a little as she glanced back at Paul. He seemed to have no idea what to do under these circumstances. Clearly Thibbony's identification and acceptance of her had taken him by surprise as well. She was more concerned about what Delgado might do—and about what Paul ought to do, but she had no way to tell him without alerting Delgado, who had not been expecting her to arrive, but dared not reveal that fact.

Thibbony eased her along, and held the door for her. It closed on the helpless shrug she directed at Paul.

After passing along a hallway inlaid with alcoves adorned with paintings, statuary, and other *objets d'art*, Yoelin found herself in a well-appointed office larger than Delgado's. The plush sofa of purple velvet looked new, as did the matching stuffed chair; both rested in front of the great desk, a throwback to the days when corporate executives had offices and actually performed their duties in them. This office, however, was meant primarily to receive visitors and to afford a measure of solitude. Yoelin found herself wondering just how much power Delgado had usurped in his role as executive secretary.

"Wren was asking about you," said Thibbony, as they made themselves comfortable on the sofa. "Would you like some towels? I usually have some brought in this time of day."

"Towels," Yoelin repeated, frowning.

Thibbony pulled out his Palmetto, his deep-set gray eyes squinting at the numbers and symbols. "And some cream for it," he added, and started to key a code.

"You mean coffee," she said.

He paused. "Yes, of course. What did you think I said?" He gave a dry laugh. "All that reading must have addled your hearing. Defoe, as I recall, right?"

Yoelin's mind raced, but without destination, as she fought to stay with his changes of topics. "Yes, Defoe," she muttered. "No coffee just now, Dad. And what did—?"

"What happened to Poppa?"

Yoelin blinked, and shifted gears. "It must be my reading," she told him, and laid a hand on his arm. "Sorry, Poppa. What did Wren have to say?"

"Well, you two are going to get married after you graduate," Thibbony reminded her, somewhat peeved. "What do you think he had to say? My stars, girl, he is focused! How are classes? The Brontës, and that Austen writer?"

"Defoe, Poppa. Daniel Defoe."

"Ah, yes, Lilliput and all that. Are you sure you won't have some towels?"

"Quite sure, Poppa," she replied, finally adjusting to her role. She found a kind expression for him. "I just stopped in to see how you were doing. I have a class this afternoon, and I thought a walk in the garden would set my mind at ease." She got up, bent down, and gave him a peck on the cheek. "I'll stop by after classes, if you like."

"That would be nice, my dear," he said, and began fiddling with his Palmetto.

Yoelin closed the door gently behind her. Sadness and pity fought for control of her emotions as she made her way back to Delgado's office, but neither won—she was concerned for Paul. When she reached the office, she found it empty.

Her heart leaped into action as she looked around for anything that might indicate where Paul had gotten to: a note, perhaps, or his Palmetto with a message in the monitor, *anything*. With trepidation, she also examined the office for signs of a struggle, but nothing appeared to be out of place or dislodged. It was as if Paul and Delgado had gone out for—and here she winced at the inappropriate memory— towels.

With a hip perched on a corner of Delgado's desk, Yoelin dug out her Palmetto and tried to raise Paul. His voice messaging responded immediately, without ringing through. It was not like him to shut down the connectivity, especially while away from his corporate duties. In the vague hope that he might have contrived to leave a voice mail for her, she tried to check his messages, but was blocked, as she expected, by a security code.

Her jaw muscles tightened. *Paul, where are you and what's going on?*

She shifted position on the desk, scooting onto it so that her lower legs dangled over the edge of it. A few deep breaths, in through the nose and out through the mouth, helped her establish a meditative state. Eyes half-lidded, she waited while her mind cleared of all thoughts and images. Then she made notes. Office, check. Desk, check. Window with curtains, check. Temperature comfortable, check. With her surroundings now set aside, she allowed events to filter one by one back into her consciousness.

Fearing exposure, Delgado had fled. Check. But exposure for what? She set the question aside. He had taken Paul with him. What could he gain by that?

She waited.

Well, he could gain a hostage for negotiations. But what might he gain through negotiations? She set that question aside.

A light thump on the floor above registered. Check. She started to set the sound onto her pile of surroundings that did not signify, and paused. Could Delgado have taken Paul upstairs? If he had, why? That area was reserved for habitation and family activities. No, Delgado had to have taken Paul outside. Outside to the airfoils docked there.

Of their own accord, her upper incisors began to gnaw at her lower lip. Her body swayed gently, forward and back, in time with a silent music. She let her memory pass back over her arrival at the estate. The image of the airfoils, docked west of the colonnade. Count them. Five. One silver, two blues, a gold and a green.

Yoelin blinked herself back. She was sitting on a desk in an office. Delgado's desk and office. She needed to go outside and count the airfoils. Counting the one she'd confiscated from her would-be abductors, there should be six.

Her running footfalls echoed throughout the receiving room. Her shoes left scuff marks on the glistening hardwood floor. She yanked open the door on the left and thrust herself through and down the steps. And counted . . . to five. The silver airfoil was missing.

Even though she had anticipated as much, the missing airfoil depressed her to the point that her knees began to fail her. The sun, on its way toward the horizon, passed behind a cloud, a temporary respite from the heat. She followed the flagstone walkway until she reached a bench by the pond, where she sat down facing the water, unable to think clearly. There was no place for her from which to plan an operation. She knew neither the opposition nor the rules of engagement. Her only possible ally was dodgy at best in his lucid moments, and of questionable reliability. Idly she wondered who would replace the missing Delgado as executive secretary. Surely a hierarchical procedure existed to fill vacancies.

The pond rippled as some underwater denizen rose to snag an aquatic insect. The movement reminded her of Ellie, and for a moment she was tempted to summon the sea dragon on Havelox Rest. But Ellie was bonded only to her, and would find it daunting to sift through the random thoughts of billions of humans for one in particular. In time, perhaps over centuries, Ellie might locate Delgado and read his purposes—

"Or Paul," Yoelin said abruptly, now thinking aloud. "What if he went willingly with Delgado? What if he's playing a long game?" She turned her thoughts inward and whispered, "Ellie?"

The Nieuws children are fine. They attend a small school.

"What am I to do, Ellie?" asked Yoelin.

You are distraught. Pause and breathe. You will see what to do.

Yoelin sighed. Ellie was right: because of her relationship with Paul, she had gotten too close to the details. She had to back away from these Rescues and view them dispassionately, from outside.

She ran her fingers over the Palmetto monitor, thinking. Paul's message center required a security code. A sardonic smile crossed her mouth as one occurred to her. She keyed in her name, and gained access. It was immediately evident that Paul did not save his back messages, only the most recent. None of them bore suspicious origins. Two were from Paul's wife. With the uneasy feeling of having been caught peeking into someone else's closet, Yoelin called up the first one, without activating voice. Originating two days ago, it read, simply:

JUST GOT BACK. GOT A SPLINTER NEAR MY EYE, HAD TO SEE CLINIC. WHERE ARE YOU?

The second was dated last night, and Yoelin felt a spider scurry up her spine as she looked it over.

WHERE THE HELL ARE YOU??? IF YOU'RE OUT WITH THAT BITCH, YOU'RE IN TROUBLE, YOU BASTARD. I'D BETTER HEAR FROM YOU OR SEE YOU TOMORROW, OR ELSE!!

Yoelin closed the message account and let her eyes take in the surface of the pond. A water lily trembled as something brushed against the roots. She heard a splash, and watched the ripples spread from it. A fish, perhaps, surfacing only to be startled by her presence. She understood the disturbances; they paralleled some of the events of the last couple days of her own life. But the lily returned to tranquil stillness, and the fish to its watery abode. In the pond, normalcy ruled.

Yoelin gave herself a tiny nod: right, then.

Clewthe could wait; so could the killer of her clients. She chided herself for not having seen earlier the one question she should have asked. Why did Delgado want *her* found?

"To kill me," she answered aloud.

Okay. But why?

That stumped her. She had no biological connection—or any connection whatsoever—with the Thibbony Family. Surely Delgado knew that.

What if he *didn't* know that? What if he couldn't be sure?

Nausea swept over her as she suddenly realized that Morrainee Thibbony might well be dead, murdered, her body most likely dumped into the ravine.

Delgado was killing off all possible heirs. With the passing of Aramis Thibbony, he would succeed to the reins of power. And dotty Aramis was on the way out, which meant Delgado was running out of time to establish his primacy.

Moreover, Delgado had no help in the estate house, else he would have sought it there instead of running away. Which meant that she might find an ally within, once she proved she could be trusted. And there was but one way she could find such a person.

Yoelin raised Dannik Exeter. The Director of Corporatia Security answered immediately, as usual. His tone belied the grave look in his eyes. "Again, Yoelin?" he said lightly. "Didn't you tell me years ago that you no longer wanted to be associated with us?"

She had no desire to banter with him, even for a moment. "This concerns Corporatia *and* its Security, Director," she told him. After enabling his hologram to hover just above the shore of the pond, where the light from yellow-white Alcoda returned to strike him, she brought him up to date.

"I'll have a security platoon and a professional negotiator there in one hour," said Exeter, when she had finished. "I can close down Tiratanga Port Authority immediately with just a word."

Yoelin shook her head. "Either Delgado has gone to ground, or he'll have a way off Tiratanga. For that matter, I myself could remote the *Sequana* here and leave."

"Procedure," he reminded her.

"You have your steps, Director," she said. "I have mine. What I need is an ally here who will trust me and whom I can trust. Make contact with him or her; I'll be waiting at this pond I'd like to drop you into."

It was Exeter's turn to shake his head. "My 'steps,' as you call them, take precedence," he said severely. "The security of Corporatia is at stake."

"Perhaps I should have made contact with the stock exchange," she mused aloud, for his benefit. "I'm sure they'd like to know about this attempted hostile take-over of a—"

"You wouldn't dare," Exeter said simply. "I know you. This isn't your way."

"It's about to become my way, Director. The alternative is to get me that ally . . . and to give me at least two hours before taking action. Your choice."

The hologram glared at her. Long seconds passed. "Very well," he yielded. "One moment."

She watched while his right arm moved, his hand doing something out of the range of the hologram. With the transmission muted, he issued instructions. When he returned his attention to Yoelin, his face was as cold as she had ever seen it.

"I want to hear back from you in *one* hour," he insisted. "Warren Keller is your point of contact. He's the Assistant XS. I told him that you were Thibbony Family. That got his attention. He'll be arriving in a couple minutes from an adjacent building." He paused, and added, "Yoelin, it's your place to cooperate with him; not the other way around."

"We'll see."

"Damn it, Yoelin—"

"My first concern is Paul," she pointed out, and closed commo.

Afterwards, she calmed herself with smooth, deep breaths, relieved that Exeter had not tried to force her hand. There were things she might threaten to do that she would not actually do. Would she shut down all of Corporatia to save Paul? More importantly, *could* she do so? In truth, she did not know. But letting the stock exchange into the loop would cause a panic she had no wish to be responsible for. Not even for Paul.

Different worlds, she sighed.

Sunlight now filtered through the upper foliage of a tree, dappling her, and lowering the temperature somewhat. About to allow herself to relax, she tensed instead at movement to her right, fifty meters away. A man, somewhere in his late-twenties. Brown hair. Hands empty. Exeter must have cautioned him that she was a fillip away from a spark in a tinderbox. She did not look directly at him yet.

Thirty meters. Tallish, slender build. Good clothes: white slacks and short-sleeved, pale blue shirt, possibly from Cucchaio Brothers, an expensive clothing chain of Corporatia Products for upper hierarchs and the very-safe. No visible necktie, but he might have strung a thin bolo around the collar. Shoes, not sprayshoe. Brown, like his hair.

Ten meters. She turned her head to look at him. He skidded to a stop on the trim grass, jaw dropped, eyes wide.

"*You're* not Mori," he cried, and rushed forward, hands curled to fists. "Who the hell *are* you? What have you done with her?"

014

The questions stabbed at Yoelin like a broken promise. Exeter had told her that a man named Warren would see her. She had no doubt that this was Wren, the fiancé. Her heart broke for him. She had to tell him something, but what? Despite her gut feelings, there remained the slight possibility that Morrainee Thibbony was still alive.

Seeing her pistol aimed at him, Keller tried to stop, and slipped on the lush grass, spilling onto his back. Yoelin, satisfied that he posed no threat, put the weapon away and grasped his forearm, intending to pull him onto the bench so that they might talk. Instead, Keller yanked his arm away, and got shakily to his feet.

His voice was steady enough. "Just who the hell are you?" he demanded. "And where did you get a handweapon?"

Yoelin ignored the second question. "Someone who wants you to sit down with her," she said, her calm masking her inner turmoil. "Isn't that more or less what Director Exeter told you to do?"

He stared down at her as if about to growl. Finally his expression softened. "More or less," he agreed. "But you're not Mori."

Yoelin shook her head solemnly. "No. I'm not even a Thibbony. Please sit down, Warren. Time is of the essence."

Reluctantly Keller complied. Yoelin found him difficult to read. Was he more concerned for her identity than for Morrainee's safety? Was he already aware of her demise?

"What is this all about?" Keller demanded stiffly.

Yoelin had to proceed carefully. Just because Exeter vouched for him did not mean Keller was reliable. She needed some indication of where Keller fit into the hierarchy. "When was the last time you had contact with Tomas Delgado?" she inquired.

Keller looked as if he wanted to spit. The smooth, tanned skin of his face became craggy, as if he had aged a decade. "What does that . . . *he* have to do with this?" he shot back.

The change he underwent upon hearing Delgado's name told Yoelin all she needed to know at the moment. Slowly and carefully she selected some details for Keller that would help him assess the situation and propose a course of action. When she finished, his entire body seemed to droop.

"Mori," he whispered.

She tried to comfort him. "We don't know for sure."

Keller shook his head. His voice was barely audible, even as close as she was to him. "I've put off telling myself I knew," he breathed. "It's the only explanation for her disappearance. I know this man Darden . . . that is, I'm aware of his existence. What I don't know is who hired him to hire you to find Mori."

"If that's what Darden wanted me to do," Yoelin pointed out. "It's a working hypothesis, that's all it is."

Keller gave her a pained look. "But I don't understand," he said. "How would Darden have known Mori was abducted, and not just missing or a runaway?"

The question had been bothering Yoelin as well. "He would have feelers out in a lot of places that most people don't even know about," she told him, without much conviction. "Or perhaps whoever hired him had direct knowledge of the events."

A glimmer of hope brightened his eyes. He fought his way through his fears. "But . . . if Mori was abducted, that could mean she's still alive," he said.

Yoelin gave a tiny nod of agreement, all she could muster. "Have you heard anything about a ransom?" she asked.

Keller shook his head. "And that doesn't make any sense, does it?"

"Not unless someone is playing this very closely, and doesn't want the facts open to view," she said, more thinking aloud than in response to his statement. "In talking with Aramis, I didn't get the impression that he was fully cognizant of his position and surroundings. If he has been approached by her abductors, he may not even be aware of it or has forgotten it."

Keller made a face as he glanced back at the estate. "I know. Physically he's in good shape for his age, but his mind is uneven. When he's lucid, he's ready to pass the reins on to his heir. That would be Mori." Suddenly he lifted his head to stare at her. "In fact, *you* could—"

"Don't even think it," she said tightly.

"But it would resolve—"

"If Morrainee is still alive, and I took over in her name, her abductors would have no further use for her."

He shook his head violently. "No," he argued. "No, we could do it. We'd simply say that Morrainee—that's you—has been designated to take over as soon as it is convenient for her to do so, and that in her stead the Executive Secretary has been empowered to make decisions." He nodded to himself. "Yes. Yes, that would work."

Yoelin shifted uncomfortably on the bench. "Which brings me back to Tomas Delgado," she said, refocusing. "Where has he gotten to?"

Keller looked away, out toward the fountain. "I'm sure I have no idea."

"I'm sure you do."

He snapped his head around, back to her, his eyes bright with fear. But he said nothing, as if silence were his only protection.

"Tell me what you know," Yoelin said softly, urgently.

Keller licked his lips, and looked around furtively. "If they find out I told you anything . . ."

"Tell me who 'they' are," she said. "Let's start there."

Slowly Keller shook his head, a gesture meant for himself. His hands clasped together and unclasped. His breath came shallow at first, then settled into a comfortable rhythm. Yoelin waited while he went through his transformation. A question floated in the back of her mind: Who was he, really? Or was it just another bit of defensive paranoia meant to keep her wary?

"Delgado has people he can summon for odd jobs," Keller began quietly, with a glance over his shoulder. "You can guess what some of those jobs might be. If Mori was abducted on his authority, they would have been the ones to do it. I don't know where he finds them, or how he recruits them, but if you look in the right places, and say the right things, you can find people who will do almost anything." He paused to study her briefly. "I suppose that category would include you. Who are you, exactly? Exeter was emphatic but enigmatic about you."

"I used to work for him."

"In Corporatia Security?" She nodded. "And now?" he asked.

"I rescue people and things," she replied. "Let's just leave it at that. You were telling me about Delgado's little army."

"That's just what it is: a little army."

"What does local corporate security think about that?"

Keller made a face. "They don't know anything about it," he groused. "Or they pretend not to know. Well . . . no, that's not quite true. I think if security was aware that Delgado had outside enforcement, they'd take some sort of action. What that might be, I can't say. The problem is that, although technically security obeys the orders of Aramis Thibbony, that effectively means Delgado's orders. Especially now, with Thibbony failing."

"I don't think Delgado is in a position to issue orders to anyone at the moment," Yoelin pointed out. "Who's next in command?"

"Ah, that would be me. But I—"

"Then you'd better establish that succession at the first opportunity," she continued. "Whenever Aramis Thibbony is lucid."

"And tell him what?"

"Keep it simple. Tomas Delgado has departed abruptly on extended vacation. Thibbony will accept that. Mention that you need his appointment as Acting XS. Have a document created and ready for him to approve, before he forgets."

Keller's expression mixed respect and doubt. "What did you say was your line of work?" he asked. "And where did you get a weapon? They're illegal here."

Yoelin smiled. "That was easy; I'm a criminal. How am I supposed to commit crimes if I don't have a weapon? Now, if I were a fine, upstanding member of society here, I couldn't get within a hundred meters of a sidearm."

"You're mocking me," he said sourly.

"Yes."

Keller glowered at her.

"As I said earlier," she went on, "I perform Rescues. Sometimes for hire, sometimes *pro bono*. Darden was killed because he had signed up to approach me for a job. His murder is unrelated to any of this; his reason for hiring me almost certainly is related. I'm completing the

Rescue I'm assuming he meant me to perform."

"You're on a guilt trip," said Keller.

She nodded. "Something like that. But my motivation is not relevant. And there's another factor."

"This Paul you mentioned."

"Paul Wroclawski."

Keller shot to his feet, spouting epithets. Yoelin did not interrupt, but allowed him to calm himself.

"Wroclawski," he said, hoarse now. "Damn it, you should have told me that sooner. Delgado taking him . . . that could start an intercorporate war." He glanced at the estate. "I have to tell . . . *who the hell do I tell? Damn* that senile old man."

"Sit down, Wren."

"Don't you dare call me that!" he yelled. "Mori calls me that. No one else."

"I'm sorry," Yoelin said quickly. "I meant no disrespect whatsoever. Please, sit down. You don't want to attract attention."

He looked glum as he threw another glance at the estate. "You're right," he said, and obeyed. His chest heaved in a huge sigh. "All right, what do you want from me?"

"Where would Delgado go?"

Keller thought for a moment. "He has too much power here on Tiratanga to leave it behind," he finally replied. "There's no need for him to flee, and truthfully not much reason to go into hiding. My guess is that he's gone somewhere quiet to assess. He owns several properties, but the most secluded is a cottage on the shore of Lake Jolla. But if you're thinking of going there, my advice is don't. Sensors, tripwires, booby traps." He paused to look at her sharply. "Why would he take Wroclawski?"

She wished he had not asked. She herself was trying to ignore the implications. Taking Paul made little sense, unless he had gone willingly . . .

I mustn't think that.

She tried out her own argument, to see where it would go. "For negotiating leverage, perhaps."

"But with whom would he negotiate?" Keller shot back. "And for what?"

That was my counter-argument, thought Yoelin. She tried to answer it. "Assuming Delgado does not know, or is not certain, that I'm not related to the Thibbony Family, he still has a chance to take over if he can clear the field of me. How taking Paul serves that purpose, I-I just can't see."

"Forgive me," said Keller, "but the rules you live by are not always the rules that he and Delgado—and I, for that matter—live by."

"Different worlds," whispered Yoelin.

"I can see this hurts you," Keller went on, his voice gentle now. "Please believe that I meant no harm."

She shook her head. "No, you're right: the rules are not the same. And perhaps I am too close to this to see clearly."

"When I'm Acting XS, I could send a security detachment," Keller offered.

"Now that I know where to go, I can handle it," she said. "You're better off not knowing the details. Next question: Darden was certain about Mori's abduction. That's the word he used. If he thought she had been killed, or murdered, he would have tried to use one of those words. On the other hand, if he thought that, he would not have approached me; vengeance or crime-solving is not the sort of problem I take on, although sometimes those processes become involved along the way. So who would abduct Mori, and why? Not for money, because as far as we are aware, no ransom has been demanded. To eliminate her from the succession? But as long as she is alive, she can inherit. It's far more effective—and forgive me for saying this—to kill her rather than get her out of the way temporarily. And I can't see her abduction as a random act of violence."

"For nefarious purposes, you mean," said Keller in an icy tone.

"It seems we both have questions we are trying not to consider," she said.

Again he sighed. "So it seems. Would you . . . can I hire you to conduct a search of that ravine? I'll accompany you, of course."

"Yes, after you've assumed the title of Acting XS."

She sensed, rather than saw, someone exit from the estate, and looked back, her hand on the butt of her pistol. Aramis Thibbony was approaching them, a smile on his face. As he drew near, he held out his arms as if to embrace her. "Morrainee, Warren," he said in greeting. "Planning your wedding, are you?"

"Play along," Yoelin asided to Keller. To Thibbony, she said, "We were just discussing an administrative problem that has cropped up. You know how Wren likes to ask me for advice now and then. Well, Tomas Delgado has gone on an extended vacation, and Wren was trying to decide whether to assume the position."

"That's easy," said Thibbony, laughing. He took out his Palmetto and keyed it. Presently he said, "There," and put it away again.

"What did you do, sir?" Keller asked.

"I announced you as Acting Executive Secretary, of course. Isn't that where you were thinking? And a good job, too. I might even fire Delgado and place you permanently in his stead." He looked down at Yoelin, his eyes not quite focused now. "What do you think of that, daughter? A nice wedding present, yes?"

Yoelin simpered. "Thank you, Poppa. Wren won't let you down."

Thibbony looked out at the pond. "Going fishing, were you? It's a fine day for it. Well, I'm off to the cafeteria for some towels. I'll see you when I return."

They watched while he walked away. He seemed a bit shaky in his carriage, but otherwise was headed along the flagstone walkway toward the building from which Keller had come. Keller's lips puffed out as he exhaled.

"Ye gods," said Yoelin. "Warren, how can he mistake me for Morrainee? Do I look that much like her?"

"I think it's your facial structure and your mouth," Keller explained. "Her hair is long, like yours. Your, ah, configuration is much the same, although she is shorter. Other than the hair, I didn't notice the difference until I drew within a few meters of you. But then, I was predisposed to see Mori; I imagine the Old Man was, too." He hesitated. "If I might ask, how did you come to choose the name of Yoelin Thibbony as an alias? Surely that's isn't your true name."

"It isn't. But the origin is . . . sensitive."

"I didn't mean to pry."

She stood up. "Let's conduct that search," she said. "Then you'd better establish your new position in the hierarchy, before he realizes what he's done."

015

Standing on the bridge of the airfoil, Keller crossed his arms over the console and leaned forward. Yoelin, aware of his relaxed state now that they had gotten out of sight of the Thibbony estate, tried to fathom what had made him nervous on the bench by the pond. The only conclusion she reached was that he feared someone might be watching him and, by extension, her. Someone Keller did not want to watch him. Which meant he had not been completely forthright with her.

Instinctively, as that notion occurred to her, she adjusted the position of her pistol to make it even more readily accessible. At the same time, she chided herself for excess paranoia; a little went a long way in her business, but too much barking at shadows could lead to the same mistakes as too little. Besides, Keller's tension might have stemmed from the utter unexpectedness of their encounter.

"It's just ahead," said Keller.

The terrain became more jagged, scarred with gullies that led to ravines and to the great ravine that led out into the steppe. Trees conceal many features, but the forest divided where the scars led. Unlike her first visit to this area, when she and Paul took the two bodies out to the deepest part of the primary ravine, she now began at the head of it, pausing to rig a sensor on the console with the aid of her Palmetto.

"I've keyed it to detect . . . signs," she explained, in response to his frown and unspoken question. "It has a narrow band width; we won't have to filter out other signs."

Keller swallowed hard. "Like decomposition," he said, his voice hollow.

"Or life signs," she countered.

"Do you think . . . ?"

"I think we'll find out," she told him gently. "Let's leave it at that. Ready?"

"How could I be ready for something like this?" he complained, overlooking the fact that the search was his idea.

Yoelin had no more words of comfort. Her hand nudged the

controls, and they set out at an altitude of ten meters, high enough that the range of her rigged sensor would include the sides as well as the depths of the gullies and ravines.

They had not traveled more than a kilometer before they heard the first ping. The airfoil descended for a closer scan, and she spotted a rag-clad leg off the port bow. Keller's chest heaved, but he held back his gorge. Yoelin docked down and idled the fan blades, and climbed down onto the gravel and sparse vegetation.

Running water from rainfall had wedged the body under an outcrop of granite. As Yoelin drew closer, she saw that the other leg rested at a severe angle and partially under the corpse. There was no overpowering stench of decomposition; the body had been there for some time. As yet, nothing had fed from it. She dropped to one knee beside it and carefully, with steady pressure, pulled it out into the open. She found it to be a man in his late fifties, dark hair over a round head, and attired in the sepia uniform of Transportation Corporation Security. The fabric had faded here and there, as had the round shoulder patch of brown winged wheel on a field of beige. She glanced back at Keller and cocked an eyebrow at him.

"It looks like," he said, and stopped. After several deep breaths, he tried again. "It's Prather," he said. "Shell Prather. Chief of Security until half a year ago. We were told . . . told he had accepted a similar position with TourDiv."

"You know what that means," said Yoelin, returning to the airfoil.

Kellers calm tone failed to mask his loathing. "The present security chief is Delgado's man. Kilroy Conley."

Yoelin climbed aboard, and tocked her Palmetto. "Abby, take the *Sequana* up to synchronous orbit over Lake Jolla," she ordered. "Then—"

"Go where?"

"Abby, not now," sighed Yoelin. "Look it up, if your planetography chip isn't fully seated. I want a count of how many people are there, and I want to see the architectural layout."

"Is that all?"

The stiff tone made Yoelin wince. "Maintain surveillance and report any changes in personnel. Sorry to interrupt your daydream about enjoying a jolt of lightning."

"There's no need for you to be huffy."

Yoelin's jaw dropped. "For *me* to be huffy? Abnoba Jane, that's it! When I get back aboard, I'll . . . I'll . . . I'll send you to your room. Without supper! *Out!*"

"Personnel problems?" asked Keller, as they headed back out.

"You don't want to know."

"Security will notice your ship eventually," he reminded her.

"To be expected. Hopefully Abby will have completed her main tasks by then."

After two more kilometers, the Palmetto pinged again, this time indicating two readings. Yoelin flew on.

"Aren't we going to check them out?" worried Keller.

Yoelin shook her head. "Those are the two that abducted Paul and me, and were going to dump our bodies here," she replied.

"You're sure?"

"Yes. This is the spot . . . hang about, another ping."

Once more they descended, and this time Keller was visibly agitated. He kept muttering to himself until they docked down. The source of the ping lay curled around a massive tree root, as if deposited there by a flash flood. The body was that of a young woman, head shorn bald, attired in a white leisure suit. A cloud of decomposition enveloped her. Yoelin held her breath and tugged the body to a spot where Keller could see it. He took so long a look that Yoelin's heart ached for him.

Finally he shook his head. "It's not Mori," he called. "It looks like one of the administrative assistants on the second floor. I'm not sure I even knew her name. I think I recall hearing that she had transferred, maybe a month ago."

Yoelin returned to the airfoil. "But she resembles Morrainee?" she asked.

Keller blew a sigh. "I was trying to picture her with long orange hair," he said. "She's similar, but no, she's not Mori. Yoelin, is everyone who 'transferred' during the past year or so down here?"

She made a face, and shrugged. "I don't know. It's possible."

"I don't think I want to go on."

"You don't have a choice now, Warren," Yoelin said sharply,

powering up the airfoil once more. "You're Acting XS. It's your job to find out what's been happening to corporate employees."

He looked downcast. "With security under Delgado's thumb, I'll be removed as soon as I make a wave," he argued. "An investigation would be suicide. And who would I call on to conduct it? That task would fall to security."

"Perhaps not . . . oh! Another ping."

"Don't go down."

Yoelin gave him a hard look. "We have to, Warren," she snapped, and dropped altitude fast enough to lurch their stomachs.

He grabbed the taffrail. "Take it easy. Please."

She brought the craft to hover two meters above the ravine floor, over a broad channel of sand deposited there since time immemorial. Her stomach settled back into place.

"There," cried Keller, pointing. "It's . . . oh, God, it's a woman."

Yoelin saw a floral skirt fluttering in the light breeze that passed along the ravine. Two feet, one shod. Two legs, bare to the knees, although the skirt was long enough to cover them to the ankles. The upper torso curled around the trunk of a tree that had fallen when water undercut it. She tilted her head at Keller.

"It could be," he said, desolated. "She wore that style of . . ." He swallowed a lump in his throat, unable to finish.

The airfoil on idle, they climbed down to examine the body. As they rounded the fallen tree, Keller dropped to his knees, retching. Yoelin took a few more steps and looked over the corpse. It was that of a young woman with short brown hair. A blouse stained with blood still clad her upper body. Yoelin had seen enough wounds to know that she had been killed by an energy weapon, and the burn marks on the blouse suggested close range.

"No more," whimpered Keller, behind her.

"Take a look, damn it," Yoelin demanded. "Who is it?"

"You're very cruel."

She stepped aside for him. "Do you recognize her?"

He wiped his mouth on his sleeve, and nodded. "She's Macomere, from Personnel," he said. "I don't know her first name."

A bug crawled out of Macomere's mouth, and Keller began to dry-heave. Even Yoelin felt her stomach lurch. "She hasn't been here long," she said. "A week, maybe less."

"Why . . . ?" sighed Keller.

They headed back to the airfoil. "In Personnel, she might have noticed something awry with security records," she said. "That's only a guess, though. At least we know she didn't fall down here."

After boarding up, Yoelin took them to the previous altitude. Behind them, Alcoda now hovered low on the horizon. Yoelin risked another few kilometers of search, but the Palmetto detected nothing more of interest. Soon they reached the widest part of the ravine, and ahead the channel broadened onto a stretch of steppe broken only by random clusters of white-barked trees. The elongated shadow of the airfoil stood out onto the sand and grass like that from a sundial gnomon.

Keller threw a meaningful glance at the sun, now a fading yellow. "We'd better head back," he said. "There's about half an hour of daylight left."

Yoelin gave a little nod and swung the craft up over the starboard wall, where she had a relatively unobstructed glide path back to the estate. Thoughts of lodging for the night occupied part of her attention. She'd made no plans in that direction, thinking that she and Paul would solve the problem together. At the moment, staying aboard the *Sequana* seemed the obvious choice, and she was just about to raise Abnoba when the Palmetto signaled an incoming communication.

"Who is it, Abby?" she inquired.

"Tomas Delgado."

She brought the craft to hover, took a deep breath, and squared her shoulders. "Go to the stern, and make no sounds," she told Keller. "I don't want him to know we're together."

Only his expression protested as he turned and stepped to the aft bench. "Now it begins," Yoelin sighed. "Enable commo, Abby. No visual."

016

"You know what I want," said Delgado.

His voice came gravelly over Yoelin's Palmetto, as if he were a few steps away from the transmitter, with something over his mouth to muffle the sound. Yoelin wondered what he was trying to conceal; a sound of some kind, but what? And why?

"Me dead," she answered.

A brief silence followed, broken by Delgado. "You and I both know you're not going to trade yourself for Wroclawski."

Then he's not aware of the full relationship, she thought.

"You and I both know you won't keep whatever agreement we might reach," she threw back. "Abby, mute commo."

"Muted."

"Abby, can you patch into his signal to give me visual of him without me giving mine?" she asked. "I want to see whether the scope of the visual transmission includes Paul."

"Working."

Yoelin sighed relief; Abnoba was behaving like a pro computer. She re-enabled commo and said, "I'm not the one on the run, Delgado. It's up to you to open the bidding."

"So you want me to think that Wroclawski's disposition is irrelevant to you."

"You called me, remember?" said Yoelin.

An image flickered in and out above the instrumentation console, of a man standing before a window looking out over a body of water. The periphery was even less clear than the main focus. Two seconds of view was all Abnoba could give her, at least for now, but Yoelin saw no sign of Paul.

"The fact that you have not dismissed me out of hand suggests that for there is more to Wroclawski than meets the eye," said Delgado.

Yoelin heaved an exaggerated sigh. "I have not dismissed you because right now I have a weapon to my head, held by you," she replied. "No matter where I go, I'll have to keep looking over my shoulder. Unless," she added, "I take pre-emptive action."

"That would get Wroclawski killed."

She put a shrug into her tone. "That's not my problem. I'm more into self-preservation. One last time, Delgado, then I'll ring off: what is it you want?"

Delgado sounded peevish. "Obviously, I want to secure my control of the corporation after Thibbony expires."

"I'm really not interested in running the corporation, Delgado. I'm interested in staying alive. How do you propose we each get what we want?"

Again a hologram fizzed into view, and this time it steadied, although it was faded and flickering. Yoelin still saw no sign of Paul. Someone as evil and conniving as Delgado, she thought, surely would not kill his hostage prematurely. But she was caught up in playing by her rules, not theirs. She could see no way out that would save Paul's life.

"The Old Man likes you," Delgado said after a moment. "You can persuade him to sign control of the corporation to me. He can retire and play backgammon over at the Hierarchs' Club for the rest of his days. And you can go and do whatever you wish."

Behind her, on the aft bench, Warren Keller stirred, restive. Silently she willed him to keep his damn mouth shut.

"Ye gods," she said, with mockery in her tone. "Of course I trust you to keep your word. Oh, yes, I think that's an excellent plan."

Delgado turned around to face her. The scope of the holographic image foreshortened to present only him, hands clasped behind him. "Yes, I hired a Locator to bring you to me. I . . . doubted you were one of the Family, but the Old Man didn't know that, even in his most lucid moments. As you saw. Yes, I intended to eliminate you and thereby remove the potential threat that you represented. I assure you, *M'dame* Thibbony, whoever you are, that as long as you are not on Tiratanga or in the system to which it belongs, I have no further interest in you, nor in pursuing this matter any longer."

Annoyed by the *M'dame* honorific, which she regarded as just another form of "Mum," she made a face and shook her head, though he was unable to see it. "It still comes down to a matter of trust," she countered. "Although I do have some experience at staying alive, I have no illusions regarding my vulnerability. For this reason alone, your 'lack of interest' is insufficient as a bargaining chip. Therefore."

"Yes?"

"You will have Paul Wroclawski taken to the *Simba Café* in the Terminal and released there, alive and unharmed," she instructed. "In due course I shall collect him and return him to his wife, which I have promised her I will do. With regard to *M'sieur* Thibbony, perhaps I shall do as you suggest, or perhaps not. Either way, you will have what you want. I assume you are somewhere on Tiratanga. I give you two hours, no more. Abby, close this commo."

In the aftermath, Yoelin's heart began to pound. She felt as if she had just gotten away with something, though she was unsure as to what it was. The success of her quest to gain the return of Paul Wroclawski depended on the regard Delgado had for her. As far as he was aware, she was at best a plus-one of Wroclawski, insignificant in the political scheme of things. All she had to win over Delgado was the logic of her presentation and the determination behind it.

A glance aft made her jump; so focused had she been on the negotiation with Delgado, she had forgotten about Warren Keller. He was standing in front of the bench now, looking at her expectantly. If he took notice of her astonishment, he gave no indication of it.

"It won't work," he said, and stepped back up to the bridge, where he sat down in the starboard captain's chair. "He has no regard for your friend Paul as a hostage to compel you. Abducting him was Delgado's way of getting your attention. It's you he wants."

Yoelin's expression hardened. "I know. But it's also possible that Delgado did not abduct Paul."

"What do you mean?"

"I'm not sure," she answered reluctantly. "I have this feeling that I should be cautious where he is concerned."

Keller nodded as if he knew exactly what she was talking about. "He is your lover." His expression changed immediately to one of apology. "I did not mean to be discourteous," he added.

Yoelin dismissed this with a wave of her hand. "There's no harm done," she said lightly. "The truth is, the relationship is complicated.

The physical side is . . . honest."

"He's married," said Keller.

Yoelin did not react.

"He wants to opt out, but for political reasons he cannot do so."

She gave the tiniest of nods.

"So he says."

Yoelin sighed. "There are times when I do not know what to believe," she admitted. "And again, the truth is, if he were free, I do not know that it would work out for us. I'm not even sure that I would want it to." She made a sound of disgust and added, "And of course I'm talking too much about matters that frankly are none of your business. But I'm not mad at you for it . . . Warren. At the moment, I'm emotionally vulnerable. Maybe I needed to say things, just to hear what they sounded like."

"Quite all right. Um, . . ."

"Please, continue," she invited.

"You have less than two hours," he reminded her.

"Abby," she said. "Raise Exeter."

Again the Director of Corporatia Security answered immediately, as if he had been poised to receive her communication. "Talk to me," he ordered.

Yoelin did. When she was finished, he said, "Now *you're* the one proposing to put Wroclawski's life at risk."

"It could be nothing," she temporized. "It's probably nothing. But I-I'm not, I-I can't be certain."

"Something bothers you on a subliminal level, Yoelin," said Exeter, continuing to pronounce her name correctly, with three syllables, as if to mark the gravity of the circumstances. "You don't have enough information to go anywhere with it."

"That about sums it up, Director," she conceded.

"Stay bothered. Where will you be while we deal with this?"

"At the *Simba Café* in the Terminal. Just in case."

"Understood. All right, put Keller on, so I can get a list of names of Delgado's people."

017

Yoelin returned the airfoil to the docksite in front of the estate house, and walked with Keller toward the entrance. Halfway there, he suggested they stop for a few moments to sit on a wooden bench under the colonnade, where they had a view of the estate's dense gardens. As night began to fall, the scent of jasmine wafted around them. It occurred to her that she and Paul had never bothered to stop and smell the flowers—not that there had been many opportunities to do so. Silence had its own aroma, lulling the senses, and she blinked herself back to alertness.

"What did you want here, Warren?" she asked him.

He clasped his hands together and put them between his knees, a sure sign to Yoelin that he had no idea how to answer her question. Presently he asked, "Do you truly think she's gone?" His tone said he hoped she would not respond.

She held back, respecting the tone and not the question.

"She's very fond of the gardens," he went on, addressing his feet at the end of his outstretched legs. Yoelin took note of the present tense form, and did not remark on it. "She put in a number of the plants herself, when she was younger. It relaxed her, she said."

"Growing up was stressful for her?" Yoelin asked.

"Aramis fathered but two children that he recognized," said Keller. "One of them ran away just before reaching her majority. We presumed there were other offspring, of lesser legitimacy. So Mori was expected to take over the reins of the corporation with the passing of Aramis, or upon his retirement. The latter would seem more likely at this point. It's his mind that's going, not so much his body."

"But Morrainee balked at this scripted future," she nudged gently.

"She loves literature, gardening, planetography, and . . . well, the intellectual side of life. She likes to think. She does not want to tell people what to do."

"Would she have to do that, when she inherits?" asked Yoelin. "I would have thought she could delegate the responsibility of day-to-day corporate activities to, say, the Executive Secretary."

Keller nodded. "Yes, if she could find someone she trusted."

"Which would be you."

"But I failed her."

"What happened?"

Keller did not answer right away. He seemed to be searching his memory, reprising old conversations, and marshaling his thoughts. Yoelin sensed her own clock ticking—not that she expected to meet Paul in the Terminal, but she wanted to be there in advance, in case he did arrive. Anxiety pierced her defenses. Uncomfortable, she shifted position on the bench, though she held her tongue.

"I tried to get her to embark on a course of study that would familiarize her with corporate intricacies," said Keller, feeling his way along the explanation. "This in addition to her other studies; I know her too well to try to dissuade her from them. But she would have none of it. She said literature and geology were honest."

Yoelin smiled. "A corporate dissident."

"That's as close as she ever came to revealing her true feelings to me. She did not oppose corporate life so much as she felt it was not for her."

Yoelin considered this. "Then it should have been a simple matter of subtly encouraging her to leave," she said at last. "Surely an heiress who volunteers to renounce her heritage is easier to accommodate."

Keller nodded agreement. "But you fail to consider that many corporate hierarchs actually prefer intrigue."

"We've exchanged one form of royalty for another," mused Yoelin. "Only the pawns remain."

"Mori would have liked you . . ." His voice faded as he covered his face with his hands. His shoulders shook with his grief. "She's dead," he whispered.

Against her better judgment, she offered him hope. "We don't know that."

"I won't give up until . . ."

Time forced her to pull away. She laid a hand on his shoulder. "Warren, I have to go," she said.

"I know."

"Darden would have commissioned me to find her," she went on, her tone hardening. "I will pursue that Rescue."

". . . thank you. I-I'll pay . . ."

"Night is almost here," she said, and got to her feet. "Those Security Platoons will arrive soon. They know you're okay, but still it would be better if you remained in your quarters until this is over."

He looked up at her, tears in his eyes. She withdrew her hand and turned away before she started to weep as well.

*

Her statement regarding royalty carped at Yoelin on the way back to the Terminal. She had blurted it out directly from her subconscious, although the thought had been lurking there since her history courses at Miquelon College, out in the Fringes. She hadn't particularly wanted to study history, but the college required two years of it, in addition to other subjects that—at the time—she could not foresee ever affecting her career. And Exeter had insisted that she graduate if she intended to continue working for Corporate Security. She graduated, with honors—and resigned two years later, taking her education with her.

From her studies she had deduced that leaders of governments, whatever their nature—despotic, commercial, democratic—always regarded the governed territory and population as their personal toys. On Earth, armies raised for the defense of a nation inevitably transformed into toys pressed into service in pursuit of a foreign policy, so that a soldier did not die for his country, but because some moron had a point to make. Corporations were no different. They interfered with one another's hierarchies and prerogatives, the intrigues in Transportation Corporation a prime example. For the same reason Paul Wroclawski had married his wife, kings married off their daughters to other rulers, and accepted daughters in return for their own male relatives. Meanwhile, people like the Nieuws family scratched the ground for a rock or two that might enable them temporarily to enjoy a few good meals.

She couldn't change it; no one could. But she didn't have to accept it. In that moment, with the Terminal in sight, she came to the realization that she and Paul simply could not be. He would never tolerate her world, while she had no choice other than to reject his.

She paused the airfoil, and pounded on the console with her fist. Tears trickled down her cheeks, ignored. She blinked, struggling to bring a bleary panorama into focus. She had to ask herself whether it was the outer or inner vision that was unclear. Understanding soon began to fill her empty spaces: It was true that Paul Wroclawski had saved her and salvaged her; it was also true that gradually he would assume a position of dominance in their relationship based on the difference in their stations. She had her own battles to fight; she did not need any more, brought on by the inevitable arguments. Presently she dried her eyes, and flew on.

Technically the airfoil was not hers. She docked it in a slot; eventually someone from the estate would come to claim it. The Terminal was well-lit when she entered, and crowded now. She wormed her way through throngs toward the *Simba Café*, her emotions still in turmoil. Would Paul arrive? If he did, what could she say to him?

Rescues usually were not so complicated, she told herself. It did not help.

Hamisi was still at the café, serving sandwiches and other deli fare. Most of the tables were already occupied, but Yoelin found one off to the side, where it might have been regarded by the patrons as part of the adjacent shop. When Hamisi chanced to look in her direction, she gave him a little wave of her hand and her best shy smile. Mentally she crossed her fingers; they had not parted on ideal terms.

His arrival at her table but a few moments later startled her. Uninvited, he sat down across from her. "Your customers," she worried.

"I have help," he said. "My two sons. See?"

Yoelin looked. In their mid-teens, in cook's whites, they were younger versions of their father. A minute or so of study told Yoelin that they knew what they were doing, and she ceased concerning herself with the café's custom.

"Do you have a Palmetto?" she asked him. He produced one, and she went on, "Do a search for GuardianAngelRescues, all one word."

He ticked at his device, and swiped his fingertip across the face of it, and held it steady while he read. His expression changed from puzzled to astonished, and his eyes filled with questions. Finally he set the Palmetto on the table, and did not look at her.

"This is you?" he asked.

Solemnly she inclined her head.

"You do this, this Rescues, for money?"

"Those who can pay, pay," she told him. "Those who can't, don't."

"It says the site has been deactivated," Hamisi pointed out.

"There have been some recent difficulties," she said noncommittally. "I hope to have it back up and operational soon. Hamisi—"

"I thought you were . . . ," he said, and stopped. "I apologize for my behavior earlier," he said formally.

She bestowed a smile on him. "There was no harm done," she said. "May I order a coffee?"

Hamisi beckoned, and one of his sons rushed to their table. "A Turkish roast?" he suggested, and Yoelin nodded.

"I hope he does not collide with someone on the way back," she said, as the boy hurried off.

"Where is your friend?" Hamisi asked delicately.

"I am not certain," she replied. "I was to wait for him here."

"You are welcome to wait, of course. But you appear as if you should sleep."

Yoelin laughed. "I *feel* as if I should sleep. Hamisi, you came uninvited to this table. I cannot help but feel there is something you wish to discuss with me."

He hesitated, and sat back in his chair. His eyes told her of fear, but not of her. For a moment he averted his eyes, then squared himself to face her. "I must confess I hoped to see you again," he said. Now he spoke in a cultured tone, the utter opposite of the one he had used in remonstrance with the protection collector. "I thought perhaps you belong to, let us say, an organization. You understand?"

"*Nafahamu*," she said. "I do understand. But no, this is not the case."

"So I have just seen," said Hamisi, as a mug of steaming coffee arrived. Yoelin pressed ten thalers of gratuity into the boy's hand, and he sped off again. "There was no charge, *bibi*," Hamisi told her.

"That was for the service. Hamisi, let us say that I was a member of an organization, as you supposed. What would you have asked of me?"

Again he hesitated, and this time he leaned forward, as if about to enter into a conspiracy. "That man who was here," he said. "You know the one I mean. I wish you to . . ." Aghast at what he was about to say, he drew back. "No, I . . . no, I cannot ask that."

Yoelin sipped her coffee and found it yet too hot. But she took a second sip, accepting the pain it gave her. The pain gave her strength. "I cannot be hired to kill someone, Hamisi," she told him. "This is understood. In any case, Clewthe has more than one collector of protection money in this Terminal. Finally, he would simply replace them if they became discouraged in their work."

She checked the time on her Palmetto, and found that she had ten minutes until her two hours were up. She had hoped for at least an update from Exeter. A quick glance around the Terminal failed to turn up Paul. She drew a deep breath to calm herself.

"What *can* you do?" asked Hamisi.

"What do you wish me to do?" she countered.

Hamisi seemed to slump into his chair, as if his physical shape were based on that of his container. Clearly, to Yoelin, he did not know what he wanted, except within vague parameters. He did not want to continue to pay protection money, as much was certain. Typically, he also wished for a better life for his children. Neither of those ends fell within the scope of her adopted profession.

Or did they? He was, after all, on the verge of asking.

The time on her Palmetto now indicated that Paul Wroclawski was five minutes late. Her heart wearied of problems she could not resolve. She was about to attempt to raise Paul when an incoming signal gave her pause: it was from Dannik Exeter.

At the announcement of the name, Yoelin's heart felt hollow. With some trepidation she accepted the communication. Exeter's hard features fairly growled at her from the viewscreen.

"You," he said, "have catalyzed one hell of an intracorporate problem," he told her. "I ought to have you detained—for impersonating a corporate hierarch, for starters."

Yoelin quickly scanned the bay from one end to the other, as far as she could see. It would not have been beyond Exeter to have already dispatched a team with detention orders. "Paul Wroclawski," Yoelin said stiffly, dragging the Director back to her own priorities.

"Was not there," replied Exeter. "Had never been there—according to Delgado, who had some interesting things to say about you." He rubbed fingertips at his graying temples. "So did the people we rounded up, though not about you."

Yoelin felt a darkness set in. "What do you mean?"

"We'll discuss that later. Right now—"

She closed commo immediately, and scrambled to her feet, looking all around her. To Abnoba, she said quickly, "Abby, disable all tracking functions except that between you and this device. Remote to the airfoil docksite just outside this Terminal, and try not to squash anyone's conveyance. Then disable this tracking function."

Hamisi was staring wide-eyed at her. "What is it?" he asked her. "What's wrong?"

She tucked away the Palmetto. Not wishing to alarm him unduly, she temporized. "I'm not sure." She glanced in the direction of his kitchen. "Can I get outside through there?"

He stood up. "I'll have to unlock the door."

He led the way, winding around counters and preparation tables, to a door that evidently was used for deliveries. This he unlocked, cracked open wide enough for him to survey outside, and gave Yoelin an all-clear sign. Passing by him, she paused.

"*Asante*," she said softly. "Thank you."

"You lead a very unusual life," he told her. "I almost envy you for it."

"I will come back, Hamisi," she promised him. "And I will find a way to help you deal with circumstances here."

His smile gleamed. "One of your Rescues?"

Gravely she inclined her head, and dashed outside to the spaceskiff that had just downdocked. Even as she climbed aboard, she heard a commotion behind her: Exeter's troops had arrived. She signaled Abnoba to seal the hatch, then FasTrack away from Tiratanga.

018

On the bridge, with the *Sequana* in null-space, Yoelin reflected that everything about this mission—she could hardly call it a Rescue—had gone sour. Corporatia Transportation seemingly was in disarray, with the Chief incapacitated by sporadic senility and the Executive Secretary plotting to take advantage of his condition and assume command of the corporation. Exeter had somehow become convinced that she was manipulating the situation to her own advantage, although she was unable to grasp why he would think so. Paul Wroclawski had become a mystery; he was not where she assumed he would be: why not?

"Abby, raise Paul."

"Are you sure—?"

She slapped her flat hand on the console. "That's it! No more chocolate-covered voltage treats for you." She sighed, not quite appalled by her humor in this moment. "Abby, just raise him."

"He does not respond."

"Is his Palmetto activated?"

"Yes. He has terminated our incoming communication."

She flopped down in the captain's chair. "I don't even know what that means," she muttered. "And I don't know what to do now."

She thought back. What was that Paul had said to Delgado about a finder's fee? At the time, she'd thought it a bit of humor appropriate to the character he was presenting himself to be. But if he were serious . . .

If he were serious, it could only mean that he had betrayed her. There was no other way to interpret his actions.

"Abby, where is Paul now?"

"Impossible to determine."

That meant he, too, was in null-space.

The sense of being alone in this time of troubles bore down on her shoulders. She'd been delighted to have Paul along, for companionship and to open doors for her with Corporatia Transportation. Their love-making had been a boon to her psyche; now it abraded her spirit. Save some moments of exhilarating friction, it had, in the end, signified nothing. *Who can I turn to?* she thought absently, tapping her fingers on the console to an improvised beat. In her past Rescues, solitude had always become her. But now she was a fugitive.

"Abby," she said, and stopped.

A brief silence was broken by, *"You rang?"*

Pain creased her brow. One more time, she thought. I need to know. But she avoided the words that described what she had to know, unwilling to face them. Instead, she said, "Abby, try again to raise Paul."

"He does not respond."

Yoelin wanted to cry, but refused to. "Same reason?" she asked, her voice barely audible.

"Yes. He has terminated the incoming communication. Do you still wish to know his location?"

Do I? She considered the question, resolving it without enthusiasm. "Where?" she asked.

"He is back on Verveine."

"With his wife, I suppose," she said dully.

"That is unknown at this time."

More questions arose. How? For she had seen him last in the company of Delgado. Had the two men been in league with one another? And why? Why at least not tell her he was okay and he was going back to his estate? To his wife? And . . . and . . .

She folded her arms on the console, lowered her face onto them, and began to sob. Her shoulders trembled, not from grief, but from the effort to control it. Even in tears, she refused to surrender. Instead, she allowed a few waves of emotion to leak out. Beads of water began to trickle down her arms, taking with them the bits of darkness she allowed to be released.

She scarcely heard the announcement from Abnoba of *"Incoming commo."*

She lifted her head, blinking, her vision blurred by tears. "What's that, Abby? Who is it?" A trace of excitement crept into her voice. "Is it Paul?"

"It could be."

Yoelin made a little sound of annoyance. "I'm not in the mood, Abnoba."

"The source and location are not identified."

"If it's Paul, what do I do?" she mumbled to herself.

"I have only a limited experience from which to advise you."

"You," said Yoelin, taken aback. Incredulity and disbelief raised the pitch of her voice. "You had a romantic experience."

"He was a PVC4 Stroke 2902, just out of the factory, and immature. We spent some pre-installation shelf time together."

"*He*," snorted Yoelin.

"I would not presume to advise you based on an It."

"Go on," she said, with bated breath.

"We exchanged a few stimulating neutrinos, but Stroke 2902 wanted more. When I refused to load on the first handshake, he went into a sulk and shut down."

Yoelin was too shocked to laugh.

"The memory of those neutrinos still haunts me today."

Now Yoelin smothered a laugh. Though still shadowed by Paul Wroclawski, she found her spirit lightened. The heels of her hands swept the tears from her cheeks. "All right," she said. "Let's have that commo. Enable visual."

The face of Velanne Moths appeared in the communications monitor. On the verge of speaking, she seemed to change her mind. After clearing her throat, she said, "You've been crying. Did you by any chance lose someone?"

Her defenses pierced by the direct question, Yoelin nodded without hesitation. "Yes," she said. "I did."

Vela's face hardened. "Good. Now you know a little of how I feel."

"Did you make contact with me to gloat?" snapped Yoelin. "What do you want?"

"You."

"Ye gods, I *know* that much. Get to the point, or get off."

"I should have said that I want what everyone else wants: you."

"What are you talking about, Vela?"

Vela's gray eyes widened. "You don't know? No, I see that you don't. Very well: the Director of Corporatia Security—your former boss, I believe—has just issued an All-Points on you. Armed and dangerous, and so forth. I'm beginning to think he wants you dead, Yoelin, although I can't imagine why. A nice girl like you, so gentle and kind—"

"That's enough, Moths."

"In addition to my sister, I lost a half-million-thaler finder's fee, thanks to you. Fortunately, there's a million-thaler bounty on your head that I'm going to collect. And because the Director is not concerned about your condition upon delivery, I'd say that's a win-win for me."

"*If* you can collect it."

The remark gave Vela pause. "You're good, I'll give you that," she conceded. "You were careless on Prana, but maybe your awareness has since been heightened by events. But I'm good, too. And for a million thalers, I'm great."

"*Meow*," screeched Yoelin, and raked the air with rigid, curled fingers.

For a few seconds Vela's jaw dropped as she stared wide-eyed at Yoelin. Then she burst into laughter. After that subsided, she slowly shook her head. "That's just what we're doing, isn't it, you and I," she said.

"I have no reason to harm you, Vela," Yoelin said soberly. "I'll respond in kind, but I'm not going to seek you out."

"I, on the other hand . . ."

Yoelin nodded. "Yeah," she whispered.

"You killed my sister, Yoelin."

Again she nodded. "Yeah . . ."

A gloomy silence fell between them. The channel remained open despite the lack of traffic. Either Abnoba or Vela's computer had overridden the automatic termination that took effect after a minute without transmissions. Yoelin's thoughts raced. It made no sense for Velanne Moths to warn her of Exeter's order, and to advise her of her intention of collecting the reward. Worse, it was unprofessional. Something else had to be going on.

Yoelin moistened her lips. She could scarcely believe what she was about to say. She blurted the words before her mind could retract them.

"Vela, I could use some help," she said. "I'd like to hire you."

Vela's expression turned to stone. "You have *got* to be kidding me."

"Can we discuss it? I have coffee."

Vela mulled this over.

"Dark roast," added Yoelin.

Vela just stared at her.

"Ethiopian," said Yoelin.

Vela licked her lips. "From . . . actually from Ethiopia?"

Yoelin nodded solemnly. "Yergacheff."

Vela glanced to one side, as if to confirm a reading on her console. "Can you divert to Aequor?" she asked.

"I can be there in half an hour."

"About the same here. The Boardwalk on Tranquility Beach. There are picnic tables."

"I know them," said Yoelin.

Vela's face vanished from the monitor.

Yoelin put her hands to her head and rested her elbows on the console. What, she thought, am I doing?

She is wary, but sincere.

Yoelin gasped. "Ellie?"

The Nieuws children are fine. They attend school, and work in the tavern, and are as happy as can be under the circumstances.

"Good to know."

Runchal has begun to treat them as his own.

"Abby," she said. "Divert us to the Boardwalk on Tranquility Beach on Aequor—"

"Diverted."

"I hadn't finished. And brew up a three-liter thermos of Ethiopian Yergacheff, my strength."

"Brewing."

"And don't be petty. Ellie is a friend."

"Then why do you never give me dried fruit?"

Yoelin found a laugh. "How would you chew it?"

"It gives off aromas that I can sense."

"I confess I never considered that. When we reach Aequor, I'll put a few pieces on the console. Ellie, keep an eye on the kids. This isn't over by a long shot."

Enjoy Aequor, said Ellie.

Yoelin sat back. Her sigh hissed throughout the bridge. *Yeah, enjoy Aequor. Easy for her to say.*

Presently she got up and went to her stateroom to arm and equip herself.

019

Cloud cover admitted only a few rays of the yellow dwarf's light to reach the surface of Aequor. The bay on the west coast of Clayre, however, fairly glowed at midday, with the beach striped by the shadows of the trees that overhung The Boardwalk. The area was the poster child for Idyllic.

Aequor was but sparsely settled, extensive surveys having detected nothing worth exploiting. The crust contained the usual minerals and elements, but not in any profitable quantities. The soil on much of the three continents provided nutrients for plants that were of interest only to xenobotanists. While the land might be farmed, there was as yet no need to expand to Aequor to develop agriculture. There was, in short, nothing of interest on the planet save peace and quiet.

Which was why Corporatia Transportation turned over Aequor to its Tour Division. Aequor's varied terrain—beaches, deserts, plains, forests, mountains—invited all manner of folk seeking a few moments of respite from their daily travails. But relatively few took advantage of this, as the planet was well outside the so-called beaten path. For this reason, prices at the hotels, restaurants, and kiosks were deflated—a small profit being superior to no profit at all.

Yoelin docked the *Sequana* in the open space behind the Blennerhof Hotel that overlooked the bay, and took note of the mottled blue spaceskiff already there. Velanne Moths was waiting for her on The Boardwalk—in theory. Nothing had been said about weaponry, and Yoelin was hardly in a chivalrous mood. She slid the Kreisler Energo and the ancient .45 automatic under the belt of her black denims, and tugged the oversized blue jersey over them, adding a silent hope that the weapons would prove unnecessary. After issuing security instructions to Abnoba, she disembarked, the gallon thermos swinging gently from her left hand.

Comfortably fresh air greeted her as she stepped outside. Several people lolled about around the swimming pool, and one or two gave her an inquisitive look. Mentally she shook her head; the pool seemed redundant, what with the ocean less than half a kilometer away. She walked around the side of the hotel with the air of a new arrival, but her eyes took in every possible danger point, from the trees and the banks of rhodies to the open doorways of kiosks that fronted the boardwalk. Her fingers tightened around the butt of the Kreisler while she surveyed the tables, looking for Velanne Moths. From time to time she glanced over her shoulder, or paused before a kiosk ostensibly to examine the wares within, but she found no sign of the revenge-minded locator.

At last a glance along the beach itself found the tall woman with the cap of golden hair. Attired herself in a black shirt and jeans, she was sitting on the bench of a wooden picnic table with a view to the bay, as if oblivious to Yoelin's approach. Yoelin didn't believe it for a second; surely Vela had spotted her as she rounded the hotel. Yoelin's black boots chuffed sand as she drew near. When she had gotten to within four paces, Vela turned around and showed empty hands.

Yoelin trudged to a stop and displayed the thermos. In that moment she realized she had not brought mugs, and in the next Vela set two of her own on the table. Even so, her pale eyes blazed at Yoelin as she sat down.

"Let's be clear," said Vela. "I'll honor this truce. Leaving here, we'll go our separate ways. But I still want to kill you, and I still intend to collect that bounty."

Yoelin shrugged. "Clear enough."

Vela slid her a mug. "Pour. And I know you're armed. Would you prefer twenty paces?"

"Meow," said Yoelin, pouring.

With their left hands they made a mock toast, and took careful sips.

"Why should I hire out to help you?" asked Vela.

"That would take the story of my life."

Vela nodded. "Which explains the three-liter thermos." She sighed. "Very well. You're the prospective client. But try to be concise. I have a body to deliver and a bounty to collect."

*

An hour and a half later, Vela swirled the last of her fourth mug of coffee, and finally drained it. "I'm almost curious about the parts I know you left out," she said, setting the mug back down and waving off a refill. "If I were interested in your background, which I'm not, I'd also say you've filled in several blanks in what is known about you."

Yoelin gazed out at the ocean. There were moments in her life when she longed to have such a view forever. With the mountains behind her, this section of the coast of Aequor made an ideal place to retire. It took her a few seconds to realize that this notion was merely her loneliness talking to her. She was missing Paul. And she was angry with him. True, she had planned to thrust him from her personal life—their worlds were different—but instead *he* had abandoned *her* for his personal life. "Nobody ever said life was fair," she whispered to herself.

"I couldn't help but notice," began Vela, and stopped.

Yoelin shot her a sharp look, then returned her attention to the echelons of waves coming to die on the pale yellow sand. "I thought it imprudent to mention your sister," she said, just above the sounds from the shore.

"But . . ."

"Yeah. I just did."

"I want to know."

Yoelin turned back around. "I did not kill Danelle Moths," she said. "I killed an unidentified woman who I had every reason to believe was about to grab a weapon she had cached and kill me and my companions and/or the Director. Despite ample opportunity, at no time did she introduce herself or broach her true purpose. Had she done so, I might very well have gone with her to the Thibbony Estate, once I had finished the Rescue." She paused, and sighed. "That's my statement on the matter, Vela. Do with it what you will."

Vela fell silent for a couple of minutes. She filled her mug halfway, and took a slow sip from it, obviously contemplating her response. At last she broke the silence with a question. "Are you sorry?"

Again Yoelin faced the ocean. The sun pierced the clouds then, and compelled her to shade her eyes with her hand. Unexpectedly, a crucial moment had come upon her. Three possible responses queued up for review: one right, one wrong, one truthful. Without hesitation, she chose the last.

"Yes," she said, "and no."

She could feel Vela's frown. "I'm not sure I understand you," said the locator.

"Yes, I'm sorry that I was in a position where I had to kill someone. I don't like killing, although I've had to do it on several occasions. And no, I'm not sorry, because I did the right thing in the circumstances in which I found myself."

"That's all very facile," growled Vela.

"You asked."

Yoelin wondered whether Vela was about to violate her own stated terms of truce. Slowly she turned back around. Vela's eyes glistened pearl gray now, on the verge of tears.

Very gently, Yoelin said, "Vela, yes, I am sorry. I have some idea, however inadequate, of how much I have hurt you. I can scarcely imagine the unending ache. If I could undo it, I would do so. Without any hope of receiving it, I ask for your forgiveness."

Vela bit her lower lip. Presently she stood up and walked out toward the waves. She did not glance back, but Yoelin heeded the unoffered invitation, and followed her out to the water. By the time she reached Vela, froth was hissing in the dark wet sand at her feet. Yoelin came to a stop a pace behind and a pace to the right of Vela, and watched her shoulders tremble. She thought to hear a sniffle, and a second later Vela raised her right hand and rubbed it a few times across her mouth and nose. She gave no indication that she was aware of Yoelin's presence. A wave crashed, larger than the others, and water swept around their ankles and lower legs, soaking their boots and jeans. Neither woman moved back.

"Vela," said Yoelin.

"Leave me alone."

"Why?"

Vela whirled around, her mouth open in shock. "What sort of question is that?" she cried. "Nobody asks why. They say okay, or no. They don't ask why."

"Shall I tell you why I won't leave you?" asked Yoelin. Vela nodded mutely, and she went on, "Because you need . . . someone."

"You?"

Yoelin blinked. "If you wish."

"So now I'm one of your Rescues."

"It's a start."

Vela took a hesitant step closer. "I . . . I need to . . . to be held."

Yoelin embraced her. Their sidearms clicked and clashed. The women drew apart, not quite laughing.

Vela quickly sobered. "No more," she said.

Carefully, with her hands in clear view, Vela withdrew her weapons and looked for a dry place on the shore to cast them. After a moment, she stepped from the water and laid them on a low rise of sand topped by sparse grass. Yoelin followed suit.

Unarmed now, they faced one another.

"Expressions of sympathy and comfort should be more spontaneous," Yoelin observed.

"Ever the professional Rescuer. Shut up, and hold me, and let me cry."

Yoelin obeyed.

020

To the dismay of Yoelin and Vela, the room in the Blennerhof Hotel had but one bed, albeit a large one. It also had one stuffed chair and one writing desk with one folding chair. One cooler, one hotplate, one coffee brewer with complimentary non-gourmet coffee packs.

"Not really set up for double occupancy," Vela observed.

Yoelin grimaced. "That depends on the occupants." Before Vela could comment, she added, "You can have the bed. I'll take that chair."

"Why?"

"Tactics."

Though closed, the room had no smell of recent occupancy. Yoelin sniffed, and detected the faintest residue of tobacco smoke, but that was all. Vela checked the cooler and found a small plastic bag of broken ice in the freezer compartment. She loaded a few fragments into a plastic glass and filled it with water.

"Tactics," Vela repeated. "Meaning . . . it's more difficult to sneak around from the bed than from the chair. You'd have the high ground, so to speak."

Yoelin chuckled, and took the glass from Vela for a sip. "The floor's level," she pointed out. "We're on equal footing."

"Only if we're both in the bed."

Yoelin stepped to the bay window and pulled the curtains. From four levels up, she could see where the ocean met the sky. Only close to shore were there waves; the rest of the water was calm. *Aequor*, she thought. *From* aequus, *Latin for calm*. Or was calm short for calamity?

She turned back around. "I suppose there's room for both of us."

"Plenty of room," Vela agreed. "Are you an alert sleeper?"

"You mean, do I awaken readily?"

"I mean . . . if I should inadvertently touch . . .

"I promise not to open fire."

"Good to know," said Vela. She withdrew her weapons and placed them in the drawer of the desk, and stepped back while Yoelin did the same. Then she closed the drawer, firmly and decisively. "This truce will hold," Vela said once more. "You still have to tell me what it is you want from me. But I give you my word, Yoelin, you are safe with me until after we leave Aequor."

"There's a restaurant downstairs, just off the lobby," said Yoelin. "I'll buy."

*

Vela gazed down at her platter. It was laden with chunks of meat and vegetables stewed in a dark, red-brown sauce and ladled over a bed of broad egg noodles. "I should trust you?" she complained.

"I'm having the same thing," Yoelin pointed out. "Goulash. Dig in."

Instead she took a small sip of dark red wine from her goblet. After swallowing, she blew air audibly, set the goblet down, and sat back. "That's like a fist to the stomach. Bikaver, you said."

Yoelin nodded, but finished chewing before she spoke. "Bull's blood. Nice and hearty." She paused, peering at her across the table. "Do you always grumble about a free meal?"

Vela threw her an arch look. "With those, there's sometimes a . . . 'dessert.' With you, I still don't know what it is you want from me." She punctuated this by trying the goulash. Her expression said it was pungent but delicious.

"Told you," said Yoelin, in response to the expression. Then: "Are you in a hurry?"

"The sooner we leave Aequor, the sooner I can kill you."

"If you keep thinking that way, you'll spoil your dinner." Yoelin sighed. "Vela, I want to find out who was killing off my clients. You know my story now. You know what the Rescues mean to me. I have to get back in." She finished with a mumble. "I have to."

"For what it's worth," said Vela, "I actually sympathize. But I still don't see what I can do for you that you can't do for yourself."

Yoelin swallowed, and tongued a length of noodle from the corner of her mouth. "Sympathize?" she asked.

Vela's face sobered, and her eyes darkened as she looked away. "Killing off someone's clients," she said softly. "That could happen to me. In a way, *it is* happening to me; I've shut down my practice until after I kill you. Yoelin, killing off the innocent to get to the guilty . . . that goes against everything I believe in. I daresay it cuts across your grain as well."

"Careful," said Yoelin. "You'll start liking me."

"Well, we can't have that," said Vela, and again addressed her meal.

"The question remains as to who would do this."

Vela shrugged. "Someone who really hates you."

"But I can't think of anyone except you," said Yoelin, shaking her head. "And it's not you."

"I was wondering why you hadn't asked me."

"It's not your style. If someone injured you, you'd go after them directly."

"Which I'm doing. Yoelin, *what do you want?*"

"What I don't want is for this meal to get cold." She made a little gesture to her with the fork. "Chow down. Hmm . . . why is it that we eat up but chow down?"

"And dig in," Vela added, and did so.

Between bites Yoelin said, "Simon Mataro wanted me. You remember him?" Vela nodded, and she went on, "He was sporting a blue octopus tattoo on his forearm."

"Clewthe's gang."

"Which you'd think I would have known. But no, I only learned of the connection yesterday. Well, one of two things must be true—or even both things. One, Clewthe has finally learned what happened to Deirdre . . . to me, and dispatched someone to bring me in and complete the debt payment. And-or two, he was acting on the reward for me from the Thibbony Family."

Vela set down her fork. "If that last bit is true, that would annoy me. We locators are jealous about our prerogatives."

"But Clewthe is big enough to push it."

"Um . . ."

Yoelin frowned. "What?"

"Left corner of your mouth."

Yoelin dabbed at it with a napkin. "Sorry."

"So where are we? Besides out of bull's blood, I mean."

Yoelin signaled the wine steward, who brought the bottle, leaving it on the table after refilling the goblets.

"Good service," Vela noted.

Yoelin sat back to mull over her decision. What she had in mind was risky, but it would clear the deck if successful, or at least clear the docket on her life if not. Finally she gave herself a sharp nod.

"I want you to make contact with Clewthe's people," she said. Her decisive tone brooked no argument. "Find out what he's offering for Deirdre Hanratty. If you like the figure—and I rather think you will—arrange a meet with Clewthe himself to turn me over."

Vela's pale eyes widened. "You're insane. Suicidal."

Yoelin shook her head. "No. One way or another, this has to end. I cannot keep running for the rest of my life."

"I doubt he's the one who's been killing your clients."

"I wouldn't put it past him," Yoelin agreed. "But he's like you, in that it's not his style." She took a deep breath and let it out slowly, in short bursts. "I'll add enough to whatever he's offering to make it an even three million thalers. That's my deal, Vela."

"What about Director Exeter?" she asked. "He wants you, too."

"He'll have to wait his turn."

"You're missing my point," said Vela. "He'll pay a million for you, too."

Yoelin smiled. "He'll have to wait his turn. If I survive Clewthe, we'll talk, you and I."

"Do you think you can do it?" she asked.

"I don't see that I have much choice, Vela." She gave the locator a hard look. "So: are we agreed on the Clewthe deal?"

Vela did not answer directly. "After Clewthe and Exeter, it's my turn. Are we agreed on that?"

Yoelin nodded.

"And you'll pay me in full in advance for Clewthe," she went on. "I don't want to have to collect the other half from your estate."

Another nod.

"Then yes, we are agreed on Clewthe. We can transfer the funds in our room."

"Finish your Bikaver," said Yoelin.

*

The yellow dwarf had set on the west coast of Clayre by the time the two women repaired to their room on the fourth floor. Yoelin stood gazing through the bay window at the luminescent whitecap breakers that striped the oncoming waters. Had she been asked, she could not have told what she was thinking. The enormity of her plan left her numb. To walk directly into the lion's den . . . Vela was right, it was suicidal. But she had already considered her other options. Now, her mind emptied, she stood very still, hands at her sides, absorbed in the beauty of the view.

"Yoelin," Vela said softly, from a couple paces behind her.

She glanced over her shoulder and saw that the locator was holding her fundscard. "The basic rule of the oldest profession," said Vela, grinning.

"Get the money first, right. I'm paying half a million now, and I'll make up the difference after we find out what it is." She dug out her own fundscard, and made the transfer.

"Now you're my client," said Vela. "Feel better?"

"Not really."

She slid open the door to the balcony and stepped outside. At the far end stood a bench, and she moved to a spot in front of it, where she leaned on the rail and keened her ear to the ocean. She wondered why the water drew her to it. Perhaps the attraction stemmed from her childhood on Havelox Rest, a planet whose surface was ninety percent water. Itinerant, she missed the ocean. And the solitary islands. And the forests.

Presently she drew a maple cheroot from her pocket and lit it, two streams of aromatic smoke from her nostrils dissipating into the warm and moist night air. Arms folded along the railing, she leaned forward, the cheroot dangling from her left hand. It occurred to her that Vela could bring an end to her easily enough by sneaking up behind her and pitching her over the railing. She did not trust the locator. But she trusted her word.

"Taking a chance, don't you think?" asked Vela, from the doorway.

Yoelin did not glance in her direction. "I don't think so." She felt the faint vibrations of the woman's footsteps as she approached, and turned as she drew up alongside her, an arm's-length away.

"Maple," noted Vela. "I like peach, when I can get it."

"Want one of mine?"

Vela held out her hand. "Sure." After Yoelin lit it for her, she turned toward sea and stood as Yoelin was standing. The expression on her face suggested that her thoughts, too, were drifting. And just like Yoelin, she said nothing about them.

Minutes passed, and the cheroots burned down. The stubs were crushed underfoot; neither woman opted for another. On the balcony, silence reigned, marred only by the faint murmur of the distant waves. Without meaning to, Yoelin had entered a meditative state. She could see herself standing on the balcony from an unidentified vantage point. If hatred or any other emotion emanated from the woman beside her, she was unaware of it. She looked down. Five levels, counting the main floor. Fifteen or sixteen meters into a flower garden. Probably not high enough. She'd recover . . .

"Don't," whispered Vela.

Blinking, Yoelin turned to her. "I wasn't," she said. "I was just . . ."

"Sure."

"I couldn't, anyway," she went on. "I told you: there was nobody to rescue me. I don't want that to happen to anyone else. I can't save them all, Vela. But I can save some."

"Letting me kill you is one of your Rescues, isn't it." Her tone made it a statement.

"If you can."

Vela growled. "Let's not start that again."

"I do have one possible advantage."

"You are a little taller," said Vela. "But not by much."

Yoelin shook her head. "That's not what I meant. If you think about it, you'll see."

"Save me the time."

Yoelin looked out to sea again. "You're after me, Vela," she said softly. "I'm not after you. That means I *might* be able to choose the killing ground."

Expression fled from Vela's face, though her voice was sad. "It's late."

"Big day tomorrow."

Sadness gave way to consternation. "I didn't bring pajamas."

"I have some aboard the *Sequana* you can borrow," Yoelin told her.

Vela nodded acknowledgement, not acceptance. "Aboard the *Scarlet Seeker*, too."

"Your 'skiff is blue."

"It's a long story," said Vela. "Well, no matter. It's better for us to sleep raw. That way you can't conceal that knife in your right boot."

Yoelin smiled. "Or that telescopic *kendo* in yours."

*

The darkness arrived on voice command. Yoelin had taken the right side of the bed, with the notion that as she was right-handed and with Vela on her left, she could defend herself more easily; at the same time, with Vela right-handed, her being on the right effectively hampered her best hand. Moreover, the right side of the bed was closer to the door—a tiny advantage, but why give it up? She could tell from Vela's breathing that either the woman was on the verge of sleep, or was faking it.

"Thanks, Vela," she said.

She heard a snort. "What for?"

"For talking," Yoelin answered. "For the girl talk. I haven't talked so much with anyone in . . . years. Maybe never."

"You do know I hate you, right?"

Vela's breathing did not slow or deepen. Yoelin keened an ear to her sounds and tried to match them. But she was exhausted, and soon dozed. For how long, she did not know. Vela's whisper brought her wide awake and ready.

"Yoelin?"

". . . Yeah?"

"Have you ever . . . ?"

". . . Yeah."

"Yeah, me, too."

"Go to sleep, Vela." As punctuation, she rolled away from Vela.

But it did not quite end there. After another dozing, Yoelin stirred to a hand on her shoulder, a hand just resting there, not moving. She thought she heard a sniffle and a sigh. A while later the hand slipped down across her back to the mattress, and she thought no more about it.

021

Morning brought a frenzy of activity: shower, dressing, re-arming. Vela was all business: she had a paid assignment. Yoelin had nothing to do except await developments and wonder whether Vela would do exactly as she had been paid to do. She remained in the room while Vela went out to the *Scarlet Seeker* to make her arrangements.

An hour passed, and another. Yoelin went through three cheroots on the balcony and two cups of somewhat bitter house coffee in the dinette. None of them relaxed her. She debated whether to try to raise Paul again, and finally dismissed the notion with a snarl of annoyance. Her heart said otherwise; she recalled an ancient song, *Piece o' my Heart*, but could not recall the name of the singer. *Take another piece of my heart.* But Paul had taken enough. As good as he had been to her, she no longer saw herself as a part of his life.

That didn't make the separation any easier. Still in a dismal mood, she let her thoughts drift back to the rescue of the Nieuws children. She had caught a glimpse of her adversary then—a shadowy, shrouded figure taking cover around a corner. Gereth, the registrar at the Terminal on Nuswan, had admitted to seeing a man in a cowl and a robe, so attired despite the heat.

No, she thought suddenly, and straightened from the balcony, thinking hard. No, Gereth *did not* specify a man. He *assumed* it was a man. If it were a woman—that would bring the problem back full circle to Velanne Moths. And if Vela was lying about that . . .

Was Vela the kind of person who would deny such a thing, even though knowing how much it would hurt?

Try as she might, Yoelin could not envision that side of Vela. The locator was many things, some of them deadly violent, but if in seeking revenge she had a chance to wound Yoelin, she would take it. Vela might not even be beyond lying in the other direction, just to wound. Yet despite a couple of opportunities, she had not done so.

Not Vela, then. So where does that leave me?

If it's a woman, what other woman could hate me so much?

In that moment, the flash of eureka hit her. Before she could give full thought to it, however, Vela stepped out onto the balcony with the Post 509 aimed at her. Yoelin displayed empty hands. "What? I brushed my teeth," she said, with a laugh she did not feel.

"Come inside," Vela ordered, and stepped back to give her room.

"I take it there's been an interesting development," said Yoelin, seating herself on the edge of the bed.

Vela leaned back against the wall, with the sidearm generally aimed.

"Why don't you tell me about it?" Yoelin suggested. "Perhaps we can work something out."

Vela shook her head, just once. "No compromises," she hissed. "No negotiations. Don't even try. Slowly, one by one, take out the Kreisler and that thing, that pistol, and toss them on the floor on the other side of the bed. Then do the same with that knife."

Yoelin complied; the thumps seemed so far away. She spread her hands to see if she could get away with the movements. "Now what?" she asked.

Vela eyed her like a shrike. "You're worth five million to Clewthe," she said, savoring the words. "That's if you're dead. Another two if you're alive when he gets here and can kill you himself. If I had to guess, I'd say he's been building up a mad for the past what, twenty-four years? That's a lot of pissed-off momentum. Oh, and incidentally, he didn't send Mataro after you. It seems Mataro took it on his own as a measure to ingratiate himself with Clewthe. I did ask."

Figuring to torment me with the knowledge, thought Yoelin. Aloud, she said, "So he's coming here, then. But you're violating your contract with me, Vela. Word might get around."

Vela shrugged. "Not from you. The way I see it, five million cancels our agreement. On the other hand, there's no difference for you to make up. You should be pleased."

"How long do I have?" asked Yoelin.

"An hour. Maybe a bit more. You know how busy he is, counting the loot and all that. Just relax; you haven't a chance. Just so you know, I'm not greedy; I'll settle for five if that's how it's written."

Yoelin shrugged, and stretched her legs, again a test of movement.

"If at all," she said.

"Meaning?"

"Clewthe could kill us both and save the money. He *is* greedy. When he makes a deal, he expects to be paid, no matter what. That's why he's been after me for so long."

"No more talking."

"You're just going to stand there?"

"And you're just going to sit there."

Yoelin drew her legs against the side of the bed. From that position, given an opportunity, she might spring into action. Not that it would do much good against Vela; she was a pro.

There was nothing for her to do but wait, so she waited. Every so often she tightened and then relaxed her leg and arm muscles, so that if the moment came, they would obey her without delay. She slowed her breathing until she could feel her heartbeats. She stretched a couple more times, testing the range of motion she could get away with. She brushed her long black tresses from her shoulders; her hair length was always a combat liability, but she was loathe to cut it back.

She pondered the why of that, and concluded it stemmed from the fact that Paul liked long hair on a woman. That meant it was time to cut it, if she lived long enough.

"You're thinking too much," said Vela.

"Is it worth two million to stop me?"

Vela drifted to the front door, putting herself another step away from Yoelin. "Think away," she sneered.

Minutes passed. Yoelin tried to keep track of them, but under duress time tended to telescope. Perhaps half an hour had gone by, perhaps—even probably—more. Vela remained tense and vigilant despite her relaxed demeanor. Yoelin wondered whether Clewthe would kill her right here in this room. It appeared that he had no other, temporary, use for her, but if she could convince him otherwise, she might live to a better opportunity. Eyes half-lidded now, she continued her breathing.

Like a cave-in, the opportunity arrived without warning. The front door slid open to reveal a housemaid. Deprived of her support, Vela stumbled back a step. The maid cried, "Oh!" and then screamed when she saw the sidearm. Legs uncoiling like released springs, Yoelin launched herself at Vela. The locator tried to bring the Post back to bear, but already Yoelin was under it. Her head rammed the nerve center just below Vela's breastbone. Air puffed. Vela's right knee came up to return the favor, but Yoelin twisted aside. The Post fired, and a black spot appeared on the far wall.

The housemaid screamed again, and fell down in the hallway. With a strength born of desperation, Yoelin brought her head up into Vela's face with a satisfying thump. The blow knocked Vela sideways, and her head slammed against the doorjamb. Yoelin followed up with a blow from her left elbow to just behind Vela's right ear, and the locator collapsed, bleeding from her nose. Yoelin caught her, and eased her across the room and onto the bed. Only then, with Vela disabled, did she allow her chest to heave as she gasped for breath.

The housemaid was struggling to her feet. Hand to her scarfed head, she staggered against the doorway, and righted herself.

"Are you okay?" asked Yoelin.

"I thought . . . the room empty," she said, in an accent Yoelin could not place. "It is past check-out."

"We've decided to stay another day." She handed the woman a hundred-thaler note, which was readily accepted. "Please forgive us, ask no questions, and forget what has transpired here."

Nodding profusely, the maid tucked the bill into the breast pocket of her blouse. "It is forgotten. But please remember to extend your registry, or I will be in trouble for not doing the room."

"Understood," said Yoelin, waited until the maid had entered the next room before moving away from the door.

Already Vela was stirring on the bed. Swiftly Yoelin recovered her knife and cut strips from the sheet, twisting them together for a rope that she used to bind Vela's hands and ankles. By the time she finished, the locator had recovered. She writhed against her bonds, without effect. She tried to kick both legs at Yoelin and missed. Finally she settled back on the bed, her eyes volcanic as she glared at Yoelin.

Yoelin said nothing; their reversed positions were eloquent enough. She glanced in either direction down the hallway, but as yet there was no sign of Clewthe. She had viewed holograms of him before—burly, about her height and twice her width, neatly trimmed black hair and beard, a nose that had been broken on a few occasions, thick lips. In a few of the 'grams he had been wearing an outsuit tight enough to accentuate his chest and arms. He was known to favor the latest model of the Lockbar, which suited someone of his bulk. If he fired it at Vela, he might also kill people in the next three stayrooms.

She doubted Clewthe would come alone. Not that he was known to be secretive or paranoid, but he rarely strayed outside his province on Spakone. He had enough minions to do his bidding everywhere, and enough muscle to enforce his will.

Yoelin sighed. Just because Clewthe had said he would show up, didn't mean he *would* show up. Her efforts might be in vain. But someone would come; of that, she had no doubt.

Blood continued to trickle from Vela's nose, but other than to lick a few drops from the corner of her mouth, she ignored it. Hot eyes continued to pierce Yoelin. She went to the 'fresher and dampened a hand towel, then moved to the bed and dabbed at Vela's nose, finally pressing the cold towel against it in an effort to stanch the bleeding. All the while, Vela issued muted angry noises. Aware of passing time, Yoelin folded the towel lengthwise and tied it around Vela's head, a gag to prevent her from crying out a warning. Vela's eyes now smoldered, and under the towel her mouth worked.

Yoelin returned to the door and checked the hallway. It was still empty.

Time. How much of it remained to her? What if Clewthe showed with lots of help? What sort of deal had Vela really made with him? She put her hands to her head; her body shook. This wasn't one of her Rescues. Clewthe's gang was stronger than most security forces— which was why his activities were tolerated. Exeter and Corporatia Security could deal with him, but would they? They hadn't yet seen fit to, or been ordered to.

She took a deep breath and let it out raggedly. She did have a plan . . . but could she carry it off?

Don't doubt yourself.

She studied Vela, twisted on the bed. As if realizing the futility of her anger, the locator had stopped glaring. Her pale eyes widened at the same time Yoelin heard a sound at the end of the hallway. Someone was coming.

Yoelin dug out her fundscard and held it and her Kreisler ready as she stepped out into the hallway. Two men were approaching, one tall and rail-thin, the other squat and muscular. Her heart sank; neither of the men was Clewthe.

They paused, eyeing her weapon, fingers curled around their own. She hoped neither of them had seen Vela during the arrangements. Everything now depended on what they had been told to expect. "My arrangement is with Clewthe," she said.

The squat man grunted. The tall one said, "He's not coming. Where's Hanratty?"

Yoelin raised her fundscard. "Transfer first," she told them. "No, don't come get it." She flipped the card out onto the floor. "Fill it up," she said, with a nonchalance she did not feel.

The squat man retrieved it. The tall man said, "You're careful."

"I'm alive," Yoelin told him.

The squat man took out a card of his own, and ticked off numbers. Moments later, satisfied, he tossed the card back to Yoelin. Cautiously she picked it up, and held it up to where she could examine it while she watched them. After a moment, she cast it back onto the floor.

"The deal was for seven," she said.

"Not until we've seen the merchandise," said the tall man.

Yoelin pretended to consider this, and gave a careless shrug. "Fair enough," she said. She moved to the other side of the hall, where she could watch both Vela on the bed and the two men. "Have a look."

They peered into the room. On the bed, Vela squirmed, her muffled voice filtering through the towel across her mouth.

The tall man pulled back a little, and turned to Yoelin. "Hanratty's supposed to have dark hair," he said.

Yoelin nodded. "She's in disguise. That's one reason why it was so difficult to locate her."

"Yeah," he said slowly. His hand tightened around his sidearm as he voiced his doubts. "You know what I'm thinking?"

Yoelin fired twice in rapid succession. Both men collapsed onto the floor at the same time, dead before they hit.

"Yes," said Yoelin, clipping the Kreisler. "I know what you're thinking."

After recovering her card, she dragged the two bodies into the room and closed the door, grateful that the maid had not emerged from her maintenance work. Vela's eyes were even wider, but she had ceased her mewling. Yoelin held the card where she could see it.

"Couldn't get the other two million," she said, and undid Vela's gag.

"You *are* insane," gasped Vela. "Now Clewthe will be looking for me as well."

"Perhaps. At any rate, the agreement I had with you is voided. I'll have to try another tack. But not now."

"What are you going to do?"

Yoelin gave a dry laugh, and fixed her with a stare. "I think we're past sharing information, don't you? You double-crossed me, Vela. How can I ever trust you or believe you again?"

"I guess . . . you can't," Vela said contritely. "For what it's worth, I'm sorry."

"Sorry you did something deliberately, with malice aforethought? I don't buy it, Vela."

She went over to the chair and sat down, and lit a cheroot. Smoking relaxed her, but she wished she also had a drink. A blend would do, but a single malt would be better. There were bottles aboard the *Sequana*, but she was not yet ready to leave.

"I thought you would let them kill me," said Vela. "I would have let them kill you."

"Would you, truly? And forego that pleasure yourself?"

Vela sighed. "No. But I'm trying to say something."

"So say it."

"You didn't have to save my life."

"Yes, I did."

"I see," said Vela. "One of your Rescues."

Yoelin made a face. "I don't think it counts if I put you in a position where you need to be rescued. It would be like a doctor breaking your arm so he could set it." She slumped against the chair and stretched out her legs. With the adrenalin rush now in remission, she felt numb and drowsy. Only the woman on the bed kept her awake. Something Vela had done nosed its way into her thoughts, but it took her a few moments to grasp it and hold it up to the light.

When she fully looked at Vela again, her voice was devoid of any rancor. "Vela, last night your hand was on my shoulder."

Vela was aghast. "It certainly was not!"

"Okay."

"Wait . . . why would you say such a thing?"

"Why would I, Vela?"

". . . Maybe I was dreaming," Vela conceded. "Maybe I did it in a dream." She looked puzzled. "Why does it matter?"

"I guess it doesn't." Yoelin got to her feet and headed for the door. "I'm sure you can free yourself, Vela. By the time you do, though, I'll be gone from Aequor. I think I know now who was killing my clients, but I have some things to check on first. I suppose I'll have to keep looking over my shoulder for you, but I can live with that." At the door, she paused for a last look at Vela. Her heart seemed to slow, as if saddened. She found herself wanting to say something more, but the words refused to come forth.

She closed the door behind her.

022

Although Lowella was the headquarters for Corporatia Resources, the planet itself possessed only meager potential for mineral or agricultural exploitation. The main building itself was located in the city of Sanaama on a bay on the east coast of Columbia, the only northern continent. It housed a minimal staff, technology making a rigidly centralized location for corporate activities unnecessary. A hierarch might recline in his boudoir on one world, and manage his office on another. Still, a few hierarchs had retained the habit of going to work each day, and the Resources headquarters accommodate them as well.

Yoelin docked the *Sequana* in the Visitors' Hangar at Sanaama Spaceport and made for a small coffee shop near the Terminal, there to gather her thoughts once more. She was scarcely able to credit her own suspicions. She needed hard evidence—and she was willing to pay for it. She'd brought with her fifty thousand thalers in bills of various denominations, secreted in the pockets of her black cargo jeans. The hem of her oversized blue jersey hung well below her belt, and concealed her weapons and a few small tools of possible use, including a decoder for breaking passwords.

During the Track to Lowella, Yoelin had instructed Abnoba to change the 'skiff's transponder signal, while she herself had selected a new identity from a bin in her stateroom, that of Jane Elspeth Kerr, ostensibly a tutor of middle-class children. Innocuous, and harmless. With her DNA secured in the classified files of Corporatia Security, she might pass herself off as anyone. In addition, the new identity helped her avoid discovery by Exeter's security teams.

She paid for the coffee with a fifty-thaler note and sat at a front window to pretend to watch passers-by, while her million-mile gaze reviewed what she hoped to accomplish. Someone in the Terminal maintained records of arrivals, departures, and routes. As much was routine at most corporate headquarters. Routine, too, was the relatively low pay for clerical and administrative personnel at the bottom rungs—

which meant some of them might be willing to augment their salaries. The trick was to find one low enough to stay bought, yet high enough to have access to the information she sought. Failing that, she had no recourse except to try the direct approach, which, if she were wrong, would prove at the very best, embarrassing, and more likely far worse.

The coffee mug was empty; Yoelin could not recall finishing it. The plastic mug and the paper napkin went into their respective recycle bins. She waved a friendly hand to the keeper and headed across the tarmac for the squat concrete building with the lighted sign over the entrance that identified it as the Terminal. Once inside, she found the usual kiosks and cafés and groupings of people, and along the left wall an administrative counter where one could arrange transportation, lodging, and meals, or file a claim or register a complaint. None of the windows had signs indicating that their functions were specialized. Yoelin wanted a window as far away as possible from everyone else, and found it at the far end of the admin counter.

Yoelin had hoped to find a man working the window; more often than not, they were surly, but a smile and a bit of cleavage opened many doors. Instead, she found a young woman in service, short and plain, her lank, straw-yellow hair limp over her shoulders, and with a bored expression on her face. But Yoelin found a bit of luck: the woman was probably into her last trimester of pregnancy.

Yoelin shook her head and clucked sympathetically. "I see they still have you working," she said. She did not have to identify "they."

"Yeah."

"Eila Wanhainen," she said, reading the woman's name tag affixed to the left breast pocket of her pink outsuit. "Finnish?"

Eila shook her head. "Ancestry only," she said. "Third generation, northern Sweden."

Yoelin smiled. "Jane Kerr. Fourth generation Scotland. And I'm sorry. I didn't mean to be nosy."

"Oh, that's quite all right. You're actually the first person who has ever said anything about it." She glanced aside, as if looking for the supervisor. "Um . . . how can I help you?"

"Oh, right. Ah, I'm trying to track down a 'skiff that homes here," Yoelin said easily. "The *Birchfield?*"

"The *Birchfeld*," Eila corrected. "Yes, I know it, but I really can't give out any information unless you have official status."

Yoelin found a crestfallen look for her. "Oh."

"I'm sorry."

Yoelin fell pensive for a moment. She looked in either direction, and leaned forward. "I could, you know, make it worth your while."

Eila blinked, and again her eyes scanned about for the supervisor. "I don't know," she hedged. "Maybe . . . what exactly do you want to know?"

Yoelin peeled five notes from her right front pocket and palmed them onto the counter top, where they were almost hidden from view. The denomination of each was five-hundred. "All I want is travel routes for the past ten days," she said. "I've reason to believe the owner has lost something of value, but I want to be sure it's the right person. I'd rather not be any clearer."

Eila licked her lips, and her eyes dropped momentarily to the notes and their denomination. Her fingers tapped out a command on the keyboard embedded in the counter, and she watched while data scrolled up on her viewscreen. Yoelin slid the money closer to Eila, who curled it up in her hand and unobtrusively tucked it into her pants pocket.

"That should help with the baby clothes," said Yoelin.

Eila smiled. "And more. Thank you. Ah, yes, there was some activity during that period. A four-day trip to . . . hmm, that's an odd journey. Um, Nouvelle Bordeaux, Zarzamura, and then Nuswan," she finished.

"Thanks," said Yoelin, who now felt nothing of the sort. "That's what I wanted to know."

"And a trip to Tiratanga three days ago, returning the same day."

Silently Yoelin swore. She should have grasped it sooner: Mataro had said he wanted her alive. Therefore, he would not have fired a beam into the beads across the door of that kiosk. That meant . . .

"Are you all right?" asked Eila. "You look a little pale."

Yoelin shrugged it off. "Probably the change in climate." She dug into her pocket and came up with another thin sheaf of currency. "For the baby," she said, and passed it covertly to Eila.

Yoelin needed to sit down. The information given her by Eila was exactly what she had hoped not to hear; especially that last bit. It changed everything. She wanted to cry, and dared not attract attention by doing so. Here, now, she wanted to be a non-entity, whom no one remembered. Even Eila would disclose nothing. She withdrew inside herself and shuffled to a bench next to a garden of artificial flowers, where she flopped down and leaned back, looking like nothing so much as a weary traveler glad to have finally arrived. It was as good a place as any to hide in plain sight.

Presently she stirred enough to feel the need for a beverage, and got to her feet. Nearby stood a small kiosk for refreshments. She bought a cold bottle of some fizzy orange drink, and sipped it as she looked around from the shelter of an indoor tree, also artificial—an oak, she concluded it was supposed to be, or an oak analog. With so much natural beauty on this or on most any settled world, she found the imposition of plastic life forms disheartening. Surely there were living plants that would thrive indoors. In a down mood now, despite the liveliness of the orange-colored drink, she wondered what sort of people would appreciate the fake plants—and did that appreciation extend to relationships?

Because she was now beginning to think that she had been in a contrived relationship.

After mulling over this notion, she made a little sound of disgust, and finished her drink. Outside the sky was darkening—Lowella's white sun was setting. Yoelin urged it to remain above the horizon for just a bit longer. She wasn't ready, she wasn't—

You'll be fine. It's just another confrontation.

She sat up straight, blinking. "Ellie?"

Your favorite sea dragon, speaking.

"My *only* sea dragon."

Your speaking to me aloud may make people wonder.

"Let them wonder. Ellie . . ." She paused, fiddling with her empty bottle. "Ellie, how much do you know?"

We are bonded; I know everything. You talked about yourself to Velanne. She is very conflicted, you know.

Yoelin sighed. "I know."

But there are murky places in your past.

"Murky? Perhaps that is a blessing."

Murky like the waters off the shoals around Otmyel. You see glimpses of objects that are not real. Then you hit the sand bar, not seeing it.

"I'm not sure I follow, Ellie."

Have you ever had the feeling that you were not you?

Yoelin recalled a few events from her years as an adolescent courtesan. "A feeling that I wish I were not me, yes."

Perhaps you weren't.

Yoelin started. "What? What does that mean? Ellie?"

It's time for the Nieuws children to go snorkeling.

"Ellie!"

But there was no further reply.

Yoelin continued to sit, erect and rigid. Ellie's words left her flabbergasted. What could she possibly mean? It was all so . . . murky. Like the Otmyel shoals. But Ellie had given her courage; she had a friend.

Now, with the sunset, the moment for the confrontation with her adversary had come. She went outside and looked for a conveyance for hire. At her summons, an airfoil floated to her. She boarded up, gave the operator a destination, and settled back to empty her mind of all thoughts save those of what she now had to do.

023

The unpretentious estate house, built along lines of early colonial times, reminded Yoelin of a bungalow, not a hierarch's residence. It came into view as the airfoil operator slowed his machine to drop off Yoelin at the front gate—a wrought-iron affair that for now stood wide open—and she passed him a fine gratuity along with the fare. The walkway to the bungalow was outlined by faint glowbulbs along the ground, and eased her approach. Inside, the lights were on. Already she had decided to abandon stealth in favor of the direct approach. Her visit was the last thing they would expect.

She had planned to encounter household staff as well—a butler and a maid, surely. She had not counted on Paul answering the front door. He stared at her as if wondering who she was, and she kept silent, the more to embarrass him and force him to wonder about the purpose of her visit. After half a minute she grew tired of waiting and simply strode past him into the foyer.

"Close the door, Paul," she said, with a glance over her shoulder. "You're letting the flies out."

Paul obeyed. Astonishment and uncertainty gave him a broken voice. "Yoelin, I . . . why did you . . . I thought you were . . . what are you doing here? You shouldn't be here."

Fingers wrapped around the butt of the Kreisler, she addressed the last part. "That's why I came." She cast a look toward the end of the short hallway that led into the main room. One side was adorned with framed paintings that she recognized as prints, not originals. Two were slightly askew, and she straightened them with her free hand. "You need to speak to your housekeepers, Paul," she chided him. Fist on her left hip, she finished, "Well?"

His expression hot and severe now, he led her into the main room. It was comfortably appointed for two, with a sofa occupied by Karola Wroclawski, a stuffed chair, two matching desks, and an entertainment center that at the moment was projecting into the center of the room a hologram of two naked people engrossed in coupling. A bay window behind the sofa gave onto a tree and flower garden out back.

The startled look on Karola's round face quickly passed from flushed with arousal to pale with fear and anger. She started to reach for something at her side, but Yoelin brought the Kreisler directly to bear on her, and she froze, wild dark eyes seeking a way out.

"Sit down on the sofa, Paul," said Yoelin. Her tone made it an order. "Hands where I can see them at all times. And shut that 'gram off."

"Paul, who is this person?" asked Karola.

Yoelin laughed. She wondered whether she was going mad. "It's no good, Lady Karola," she said. "I know." She looked at Paul. "Where's your staff? And think before you answer, Paul. If anyone else is in here, have them come to this room and sit over there against the wall. Make sure they are all there, Paul, because I will shoot anyone else on sight."

"We have a cook and a housemaid," said Paul. "They are in their quarters out back. They are tending Pavel so that my wife and I may have a few moments. Shall I send for them?"

"That won't be necessary," said Yoelin. "My warning stands. It will not be repeated."

"What do you want?" Karola hissed.

For a few seconds Yoelin's gaze faded. She had come prepared to kill; now, she was hesitant. She wanted answers even more—answers to questions that it hurt her even to consider, much less to ask.

It has to be done.

"Yes, Ellie, I know."

Paul frowned. "Who are you talking to?"

"To you, Paul. Tell me why you abandoned me on Tiratanga."

Paul licked his lips, and clasped his hands together, as if to prevent them from shaking. "I was told you were dead," he replied.

"You *should* be dead," snarled Karola. "You're *supposed* to be dead."

Yoelin ignored her. "Who told you that, Paul?"

"Don't you know?"

She fired the Kreisler. The blue beam lanced across the side of his lower left leg before passing into the floor, where the carpet began to smoke. He cried out in anguish; Karola leaped to her feet and shrieked,

"How dare you!" Yoelin fired into the woman's right knee, and she collapsed back onto the sofa, clutching the cauterized wound, moaning, and gasping for breath. Mucus began to bubble from Karola's nostrils as she seethed in agony.

"That's not bad," she said to Paul. "With your money and position, you can afford a really good dermatological specialist. I'll bet you won't even have a scar."

She eased over to the end table, picked up a half-drunk mug, and cast the contents onto the smoking hole in the carpet.

"Let's try again," said Yoelin. "Paul, who told you that?"

"Damn it!" Paul yelled. "You can't barge in here like this and just shoot me. What kind of person *are* you?"

Yoelin frowned. "I thought I'd already established that," she mused. "Apparently not." With a shrug, she fired the weapon again, this time at the other side of Paul's leg. "One last time, Paul: who?"

"Delgado," he answered, through clenched jaws.

The response, though expected, served only to puzzle her. "But why kill me?" she wanted to know. "Whatever did I do to the Thibbony family?"

"I don't want to get shot again," said Paul, his voice tight with pain.

"Then answer the question," Yoelin said easily.

"I don't *know*," he snapped. "I don't know. It's a long game."

"What does that mean?"

"I don't know," he said again, this time cringing in anticipation of another searing blue beam. "I don't. I only had a small part."

"In what, Paul?"

"It's a corporate takeover."

Yoelin shook her head. "But why involve *me*?" she asked. "I'm not even a Thibbony."

"They don't know that!" Paul protested. "They think you're . . ."

"What, Paul? They think I'm what?"

"You're the elder sister," he said, and fell back against the sofa. "You're the heir." Slowly he shook his head. "You don't know, Yoelin. You just don't know. I did what I had to do. What I was instructed to do. But I . . . well, you know what happened."

"What happened, Paul?"

"I . . . came to love you," he told her. "I did; it's true. I paid a heavy price for getting you away from them, getting you to where they dared not touch you."

Beside him, Karola hissed angrily, and not because of her wounded knee.

Yoelin's eyebrows jammed together so hard that they made her forehead ache. Frustration shot through her. Understanding evaded her. Worse, she had no idea what there was to understand.

What was going on? What was he talking about? He sounded as if this "long game" went all the way back to their initial encounter. How could that be?

"Slut," snarled Karola.

Yoelin turned the Kreisler to her. "Paul," she said, without looking at him, "were you aware that she was killing off my clients?"

"What? She *what?*"

The disbelief in his voice seemed genuine. Yoelin didn't credit it for a second, but she went along with it. "I suborned a sight of the *Birchfeld*'s flight manifests. She was at Nouvelle Bordeaux, Zarzamura, and Nuswan at the same time my clients were killed there, or in the last place, attacked. She has means, opportunity, and certainly motive."

For several seconds Paul was silent. Then: "I didn't know."

Yoelin laughed without humor. "*Of course* you knew. She also went to Tiratanga, arriving there *ahead* of us. How did she know where to go, Paul? How could she take control of the *Birchfeld*, unless she had accompanied you to Prana? And ye gods, Paul, couldn't you have christened it something more . . . spacey? Or something personally appropriate. The *Arnold*, the *Quisling*, the *Vichy*, the . . . name of that Greek who led the Persians around the narrows at Thermopylae.

"Here, Paul, let me help you out. She accompanied you to Prana. You didn't have to remote your 'skiff to Tiratanga, because she was already on her way. I've thought over what we discussed on Prana; events led me to go to Tiratanga, but I feel certain that had I elected to go somewhere else, you would have nudged me, ever so gently, in the direction you wanted me to go."

"You can't prove that," gasped Paul, rubbing his leg.

Still she would not look at him. Karola was the more dangerous adversary. "Prove, no," she conceded. "But it makes sense. And she *did* take the *Birchfeld* to Tiratanga, and arrived there before us. That much, I *can* prove."

"What . . . ?" began Paul, and stopped. After licking his lips, he tried again. "What are you going to do?"

"Well, that's the question, isn't it?" she said, almost idly. "What am I going to do? I left something out, you know. The first attempt on my life at Prana, the one before Clewthe's man Mataro came at me, was carried out by you, Karola. The decision to kill me had already been made. But you were acting out your anger on my clients—on orders, I'm sure, but they were eagerly followed. You felt you deserved a shot at me. There may be a long game here, but you've been mad at me ever since you learned of our liaison. That's been *your* long game. You were given the go-ahead. The question is, why now? What's changed?

"I think it all goes back to Ellis Darden," she went on, more to herself than to her captives. "Whatever this 'long game' is, he wasn't in on it. He'd gotten wind of Morrainee Thibbony's disappearance, and thought it was an abduction, and here I was, in the professional rescue business. Unique, if I may say so, in that regard. Add that to the fact of my name, or of the name I had taken on, and approaching me was the logical thing to do.

"But whoever's behind all this . . . Delgado, couldn't allow Mori to be found. And he had no idea where she had gotten to." She paused, and gave a little chuckle. "The funny thing is, he outsmarted himself. What he really wanted was to be granted plenipotentiary powers by Aramis Thibbony, giving him effective and total and unaccountable control over one of the wealthiest corporations. But Thibbony had already given that to Warren Keller . . ."

Again she paused, and swore violently. "Ye gods, I should have seen that. He gave those powers to Warren Keller as a wedding present, thinking in his delusional way that I was Mori and that this was what I wanted. Keller played me. He played everyone. He saw his chance, and took it. Maybe he was even in on this long game from the beginning. But it was Mori's *unexpected* disappearance that set off the chain of events."

She stared down at Paul. "I'll bet you that if I make contact with

Exeter, he'll tell me that Delgado was killed in that raid. He won't realize it until I tell him, but Keller betrayed them all, and seized the golden fleece by getting Corporatia Security to clear his way. Exeter hinted as much, only I was too worried to listen." She finished with a quiet tone loaded with hushed venom. "Worried about you, Paul, you bastard."

Paul looked utterly spent and utterly defeated. "Hell hath no fury," he whispered hoarsely.

Yoelin returned her attention to Karola. "You'd better get that looked at," she said. "Medical care can work wonders, but you've got a one-centimeter hole burned through your patella. You'll spend at least half a year in physical therapy." She aimed the Kreisler carefully. "Let's make it a full year," she said, and fired at the other knee.

"Yoelin," cried Paul.

She shook her head. "No, Paul. It's over. By all rights and by the rules of justice I should kill both of you before I leave here. But I can't. It's not in me to do that. If you had a weapon, that would be different. But you don't, and Lady Karola who does is otherwise engaged.

"So here are my terms, Paul. I let you live. If I ever see you or her again in any context and under any circumstances, even out shopping, or if you ever try to interfere with my life or my work in any way whatsoever, even by proxy, I will overcome my reluctance and hunt you down and kill you. No questions asked."

Her lips puffed out as she exhaled. "Goodbye, Paul," she said, and backed out of the bungalow.

024

Aboard the *Sequana*, and in orbit around Lowellia, Yoelin leaned over the instrumentation console, arms locked to hold her up. The oversized blue jersey trembled as her chest heaved. A distant gaze passed beyond the farthest star. Silence enveloped her; even Abnoba knew when to shut the hell up. Presently she began to quake.

It's okay, she thought. *Let it out. You've paid for it.*

Cry, baby, cry.

Tears already flowing, she flopped down into the captain's chair. Sobbing wracked her. She began howling with grief, wailing out her sorrow to the rest of the Universes. Memories paraded forth, too swiftly for more than a glimpse, and with them her desires and hopes. One day, she had always imagined, one day; now an era had come to an end. She made fists of stone and pounded on her thighs. She could scarcely draw a breath. Water leaked from her; even from a corner of her mouth hung a rope of drool. Her nose clogged, and filled her sinuses. Her head ached.

Her heart ached like rock on bone.

That she had already made the decision to tell Paul that they would have to go their separate ways gave her no comfort whatsoever. Even in the shadow of that decision she had not lost hope. But now, now . . .

Her tears subsided, and flowed anew. A thesaurus of emotions pummeled her. She had no clear thoughts, and did not want any. She felt but one urge: to sit in the middle of a road like a big dumb pudding and wait for something to come along and squish her. At the same time, she knew she would not, *could* not, do that, any more than she could leap from the balcony. She had a life, and a purpose. She needed to lose herself in it.

She wiped her eyes with the heels of her hands, emptied at last, and still tears trickled.

"Abby?"

"*Yo!*"

She could not help giggling. Nor could she help thinking she was too old to emit such a sound. She wanted recovery, not regression.

"Where are we?" she asked.

"Eleven point eight four . . ."

"Points are for obsessive-compulsives, Abby. "

"About twelve minutes from being boarded by a Corporatia Security squad."

Yoelin sat up straight. "Ye gods, why didn't you say something? Never mind. Calculate a Track for Providence, and get us gone. Let's—"

"Calculated. Gone."

The stars in the Videx vanished.

"So I see," she said. "Let's go have a word with The Axe, and get him to call off his dogs." She got to her feet, and swayed for a few seconds before regaining her equilibrium. "What's our travel time?"

"One point four—"

"Abby!"

"We'll be there in a jiffy."

"Wake me when we're ten minutes out."

*

With the Videx in Zoom mode, Yoelin studied Exeter's estate, looking for anything that might suggest he had deployed armed security. The house was still under repair from the attack months ago by rogue hierarchs, but the scaffolding on the east wing had trickled down to a couple of ladders. A further Zoom located Exeter himself, sitting in the shade of an umbrella on his patio. He looked more like a tourist than the head of security for all of Corporatia.

An automated voice resounded throughout the bridge. "Attention unidentified spaceskiff: you have entered a restricted zone. Identify yourself and your reason for being here. You have ten seconds. Nine . . . eight . . ."

"Abby, raise Exeter."

His voice came through immediately, supplanting the security measures. "This is an interesting turn of events, Yoelin. I gather you wish to turn yourself in."

She noted that he clearly pronounced all three syllables of her name. "I'm unilaterally declaring an armistice, Director," she told him.

"The proverbial white flag. I'm interested in sorting out whatever this is. I'm going to downdock onto the lawn before you. Mind the puff of displaced air."

"Acknowledged. Will Balvenie do you?"

"Two fingers over a rock, please. In one of those Waterford crystal tumblers, to honor a single malt. Out."

Moments later, Yoelin stepped from the hatch onto lush grass, and made her way to the patio, where Exeter invitingly held up a tumbler. She reflected that he never seemed to change much. His eyes matched the steel gray streaks in his dark hair. His clothing—at the moment, he was wearing a white tee shirt and a pair of blue shorts that did not quite reach his knees—fit him as though he grew the fabric out of his skin. Even casually dressed, he looked like an investment banker, now on holiday on some tropical island on a world out in the Fringes.

Approaching, she slowed, looking around for any sort of treachery. It would not be unlike him to have her placed under detention, despite her declaration of an armistice. But he merely smiled at her, and invited her to seat herself in a wire mesh chair with a thick seat cushion. She did so, tugging the jersey down in a manner calculated to let him know that she was armed.

Exeter handed her the tumbler. "You might want to change your transponder back," he said.

"I've been distracted." She took a sip, and found it both warmed and steadied her. Another sip followed.

"From all accounts, you've been busy."

She set the tumbler down, and leaned back, stretching her legs. "What happened on Tiratanga, Director?" she asked.

Exeter took his time before responding. When he did, he was looking not at her but at the expanse of rolling terrain that spread to a distant forest. Yoelin had only the tone of his voice by which to gauge his veracity. It seemed likely the evasion was tactical—she had always been able to read his eyes.

"I told you earlier that Tomas Delgado had some interesting things to say about you," Exeter began. "He had gathered his own security personnel in order to counter your attempt to stage a coup by getting Aramis Thibbony to name you as his heir and place you immediately at the head of the corporation. Unfortunately, when my people arrived, his opened fire, forcing us to defend ourselves. Delgado escaped injury by climbing into a hidey-hole—"

"He would," Yoelin snorted.

"Everyone else was killed. We also rounded up those corporate personnel identified to us by Warren Keller. They made protestations of innocence, but several of them had weapons, and . . ."

He did not have to complete the sentence. "That was convenient for Delgado," she said.

"How so?"

"Those people you rounded up were actually loyal to Aramis Thibbony," she told him. "Warren Keller is a traitor."

Exeter shook his head. "He was appointed Chair of Corporatia Resources by Aramis himself. He's in charge now."

"Not for much longer."

He glared at her. "What does that mean, Lieutenant?"

"No! I'm not your lieutenant, and I'm not coming back to work for you. Now tell me what Delgado had to say about me."

Exeter seemed to stare further across the savannah. "He's dead; I think I mentioned this. Internal corporate action. In retrospect, perhaps we should have interfered."

He sighed and fell silent, and Yoelin refrained from barging into his thoughts. Eventually he would respond or would refuse to do so, and past experience said that she would have to wait him out. He sipped at his whiskey, and turned the tumbler this way and that, and did not look at her. Just as she began to debate whether she should throttle him, he broke the silence.

"Among other things, Corporatia Security maintains DNA records for every person under Corporatia control." Quickly he held up a hand to forestall her. "Yes, I know that you know this. You also know that your own DNA is in the Restricted Section of those records. Technically, as you are no longer a member of our service, some of your records should be declassified. I have taken it upon myself to keep them protected."

Yoelin grimaced. "In case I should come back," she said. "I appreciate the privacy, Director, but I'm not coming back to work for you. And you still haven't told me anything new."

"I've kept them restricted for two reasons," said Exeter. "This is not for public record, Yoelin, but I believe you are doing some good out there. I commend you for it. And that's also one reason why I have rendered assistance to you now and then."

"Which I appreciate, and will repay in my own way."

"Yes. Well . . ."

"The second reason, Director?" she pressed.

He hesitated. "There are some . . . questions regarding the DNA we have on file for you."

The statement stunned Yoelin. She managed to keep most of it from her face, but her heart rate was already increasing. "Questions," she repeated.

"It's very, very rare," he said. "But sometimes there are . . . mix-ups." Now he looked directly at her, and picked up a cotton-tipped stick from the table. "I'd like to take a swab of the lining of the inside of your mouth. I won't run the sample here; I'll turn it over anonymously to a specialist for evaluation."

She waited. "I didn't hear you say you would inform me of the results," she said.

"It's . . . complicated."

She half-rose from her seat. "Then uncomplicated it," she yelled. "I have a right to know."

"Actually, you don't," Exeter told her. "The statutes are quite clear on policy. DNA records, including gathering, analyses, and recording, fall under the purview of Corporatia Security. This practice, in theory, is to prevent identification abuse by the several corporations."

She finished standing up. "Damn you," she said softly. "Am I free to go, then, damn you."

He looked up at her, and nodded. "I called them off the moment after we broke contact. Again in retrospect, I should never have dispatched security against you. At the time, circumstances on the ground on Tiratanga were fluid, I . . . I do apologize, Yoelin." He reached out with the cotton-tipped stick. After a moment, she opened her mouth and leaned down. When he had finished, she stalked off toward the *Sequana*, her spine rigid. She did not look back.

025

Fuming failed to calm Yoelin. Once more she sat at the bridge of her 'skiff, her mind frothy with anger. Clearly at least two people knew something about her that she herself did not know. Encounters with both had not gone well. Yet she had nowhere else to turn. One other individual might have been able to clarify her situation, but he, Delgado, was dead.

Did you see the body?

Yoelin's eyes widened. "Ellie?"

The Nieuws children want to remain here.

"What about their claim on Nuswan?"

She could almost feel Ellie shrug.

They wish to remain here. What will you do now?

She shook her head. "I don't know. I think I have to return to Tiratanga. I think the truth is there."

You may not find the truth you want to know.

"What does that mean, Ellie? And please, no evasion. Earlier you suggested I was not me, and you avoided an explanation."

Ellie seemed dismayed. *I am uncertain. Oh, my bondmate, you are difficult for me to read.*

"Bondmate?"

Is that not the correct word?

Yoelin chuckled. "I have no idea, Ellie. So it is, then. What about their schooling, and a place to live?"

They have a boat and a small island. There is a small college here. Manohra Dhu has already taken on Kaleen as an assistant in her research. I have promised Runchal that you will establish a trust fund for them.

"I'll bring a fundscard for them next time I visit."

Soon.

"Yes, bondmate. Soon."

After deciding to keep to the changed responder signal and her identity as Jane Elspeth Kerr, she gave Abnoba the Track instructions, and settled back in the chair to await arrival.

Before she knew it, she was blinking herself awake to Abnoba's announcement of downdock. The Terminal assigned her a slip in the private hangar. She did not disembark right away. First she needed to establish a course of action, based on what she hoped to accomplish, and that was vague at best. She still liked the direct approach, but she had no doubt that Warren Keller would have her shot on sight. But if he didn't see her . . .

This time, after much internal debate, she concluded that once again the direct approach would serve her well. In any case, the Thibbony estate would hardly be expecting a visit from her, and much less for her to come walking right up to the door to tug on the bell pull. After passing through Port Authority as Jane Elspeth Kerr and with her armaments undetected, she let an airfoil and swept it out to the estate, docking in the site just west of the colonnade. Only two other airfoils were parked there, the so-called palace coup evidently having taken its toll.

In the late afternoon, shadows stretched, and cast the dense garden to the east in mystery. Yoelin paused before it. The darkness within seemed to envelop her as well. She might lose herself in there, if she wished. But her goal lay within the estate itself. She yanked on the bell rope.

The same butler as before, portly and balding, answered the call. His eyes widened upon seeing her, as they had on her first visit, but now he acknowledged her existence. "*Mademoiselle*," he said, with a slight bow, and she decided that was better than "Mum." Then, to her surprise, he placed a finger across his lips for silence, and gently shut the door after she entered.

A toss of his head bade her follow him. They crossed the gleaming hardwood floors to the door of Aramis Thibbony's office, and paused there. Yoelin cocked an eyebrow at him.

"There are things you must know," he whispered.

Startled, she said, "You know me?"

"Please do not speak." After she nodded, the butler continued. "*M'sieur* Thibbony drinks five or six cups of coffee each day," he told her. "They are prepared by one of the servants—Delgado's man. The

166

first cup of the day includes a tiny amount of a designer drug that clouds the mind and makes the drinker suggestible. Its effects are not cumulative, which means it must be administered each day. It has been so for the past sixteen years.

"I learned of this but two days ago, when I chanced to see the servant add the daily dose. I . . . confess I did some things of which I am ashamed, but in doing them I learned the truth. Today *M'sieur* Thibbony is . . . more lucid. He may recognize you."

Yoelin frowned. "What do you mean by that?" she demanded. "*Why* would he recognize me?"

"Keep your voice down. *M'sieur* has those loyal to him in this household, but also a few who were loyal to Tomas Delgado," his expression made the name a curse," and now to Warren Keller."

"Where is Keller now?" she asked.

The butler's face took on a sour look. "He is in his quarters upstairs, undoubtedly making more arrangements to replace staff here."

"Now tell me why he would recognize me?"

"See for yourself," said the butler, and nudged the door open.

Aramis Thibbony, wearing a royal blue dressing gown, was sitting on the purple sofa reading something on his Palmetto. At Yoelin's entrance he looked up, his deep-set gray eyes taking her in. They narrowed, then widened. The Palmetto spilled from his hands to the carpet with a soft *thump.*

"Yoelin?" he cried hoarsely, and struggled to his feet.

At the sound of her name, Yoelin felt her knees buckle. She scarcely heard his next words, or the butler close the office door behind them.

"You've come back," said Thibbony. He held his arms out to her, and she stepped gingerly into the circle of them. "Oh, you've come back, after all these years."

The capacity for thought fled Yoelin. The old man smelled of sweat poorly masked by something floral. But there was no mistaking the deep affection of his embrace. She pulled her head away to regard him. Tears tracked his cheeks.

How was this possible?

"I need . . . I need to sit down," she mumbled.

"Of course, of course," said Thibbony, leading her to the sofa. After seating her, he turned to the butler. "Jonas, a brandy, if you please. Make it two."

"Yes, *M'sieur*," said Jonas, and bowed out.

Thibbony settled for a cushioned straight-back chair, which he drew up so that he could look at her. He took up her hands in his. She allowed him the contact because it was paternal, even though he could not be her father.

"We have so much to discuss," he said, and gave her a concerned look. "That can wait. First, are you all right? You're not harmed?"

"I'm very confused," she admitted.

"What did they do to you?"

She shook her head slowly. "I don't . . . know. I don't know that anything was done to me. How-how do you know my name?"

Thibbony smiled easily. "You're my oldest daughter."

She sensed a trap about to spring shut. She, who dared not put down roots anywhere in the Spiral Arm, found herself on the verge of imprisonment. Like a startled bird, she felt the urge to flee. Her protest lurched forth. "I-I . . . No, I can't be. I can't possibly be."

Now he laughed. "I won't ask you to show me," he said, "but you have—or you used to have—a diamond-shaped birthmark on the inside of your left thigh. Your nursemaid refused to wash it until she was assured it was not contagious."

Involuntarily, Yoelin dropped her left hand over the spot. "How did you—? How *could* you—?"

How could he possibly know that?

"Ellie," she cried, adding a silent request for help.

You're doing fine. I myself am curious to know.

"Ellie?" said Thibbony.

"It's a long story." She forced calm upon herself, marshalling her courage with her thoughts. The trap had not fully sprung. She might still avoid it. If all else failed, she could fly away.

"Everything about me is a long story," she said. "I no longer know what is real and what is illusory. I don't, I don't . . . oh, ye gods. Ye gods."

"Take your time, my dear. We have plenty of it."

She shook her head almost violently. "No, we don't," she cried. "You don't understand why I'm here. I'm not your daughter; I *can't* be. What I am is a . . . a Rescuer. You're in danger. With me hunted and you drugged, the time is right for a palace coup. I can stop it before it goes any further."

Thibbony nodded slowly, and pulled his hands away. "Jonas intimated there was trouble brewing. But . . . are you certain?"

"They were going to install Morrainee as a figurehead," said Yoelin. "They were grooming her for years, and longer. Somehow she grasped what they were planning, and removed herself from the equation."

He shut his eyes for a few seconds. Finally his thoughts staggered out. "Yes, Mori . . . she . . . went back to university. But I just saw her . . ."

"That was me."

He studied her face. "Your hair. You had changed your hair."

"Morrainee—Mori has red hair," countered Yoelin. "Mine has always been black."

Jonas returned with two snifters, each half-filled with a brandy whose aroma struck Yoelin's nostrils even before he handed one to her. She took an appreciative sniffing, and smiled her approval. A testing sip made her smile grow. She waited while the butler took up a position near the door before she spoke again.

"Morrainee . . . Mori is not at university," she said. "She has gone into hiding."

"You are certain?" Jonas blurted. Under more formal circumstances his interruption would border on the unforgivable, but Thibbony merely looked at him. "You have seen her? She is alive?"

"I have not seen her," Yoelin told him. "But yes, I believe she is alive, and I may know where to find her. First, however, the Thibbony estate must be protected." She got to her feet, and set the snifter down on the end table. "*M'sieur* Thib—Poppa, I must do something that is distasteful to me, but it is the only way to resolve this. Please allow me."

His pale eyes betrayed puzzlement; still, he made a little gesture of permission.

"Jonas," instructed Yoelin. "Go and inform Warren Keller that

M'sieur Thibbony wishes to see him in his office."

As Jonas departed, Thibbony said, "Mori and Warren are getting married, you know."

"I don't think so." She took another sip of brandy. "Rothschild?" she asked.

"Of course." His expression seemed to drift. "I recall when you were but a girl, fifteen or so, you discovered single malts. You never showed an inclination to drink too much, for which I was grateful. You did show a fondness for appetizer olives, however."

Yoelin wondered whether he was losing it again. She did in fact love unpitted and marinated olives, but his mention of them at this moment felt to her like a *non sequitur*. She moved away to a spot where she had a clearer view of the doorway when it opened, and hoped Thibbony would not go off his nut and interfere.

The anticipated knock on the door arrived. Thibbony bade the visitor enter; it proved to be Jonas, who held the door for Warren Keller. He spotted Yoelin immediately, but it was already too late. She swept the Kreisler from her clip and fired a crisp blue beam into the center of his chest.

026

"What have you done?" gasped Thibbony.

A gesture from Yoelin with the weapon got Jonas to shut the door. "What had to be done," she said, with a control she did not feel. "He would have used Morrainee—Mori—while he solidified his power, and when he had done that, he would have killed her. You, of course, would already be dead. Don't forget, you already gave him effective control of the corporation as Executive Secretary."

Lines of doubt creased the old man's face. "I did that? When did I . . . *why* would I have done that?"

Yoelin took several breaths, a few to steady her mind, a few others to keep her gorge down. Presently she took a couple more sips of her brandy. "I'm afraid I'm responsible for that, *M'sieur* . . . Poppa. At the time, I thought it would save the corporation from the predations of Delgado. Unfortunately, out of the frying pan and into the fire." She laid a hand on his shoulder. Her eyes met his. "But it's all right now. It's all right."

To Jonas, she turned and said, "Can we get rid of that?" She punctuated the question by toeing the corpse.

"Of course, Lady Yoelin."

She winced. "Please don't call me that."

"As you wish, Mil . . . Very well. And as to his three supporters in the estate?"

Now she smiled. "Let's wait and let Mori decide what to do about them."

"Then you know where she is?" asked Jonas.

"I think so," she said, and moved to the door. "I'll be back—shortly, I hope."

*

Night humidity hung thick in the garden next to the estate. As Yoelin tried to maneuver around dense damp shrubs and push limbs out of her way, she found herself wondering whether anyone had ever bothered to search here. The tropical forest—it could be nothing else—

was forbidding, to say the least. But somewhere in here had been Morrainee Thibbony's favorite spot; with no paths to guide Yoelin, finding that spot was daunting.

Even the pencil flash was of little help. All she could see was the next limb, the next shrub. Whatever lay behind them could only be discovered after she passed. She estimated that she had penetrated some thirty meters when she came to a stop at what looked like a very old banyan tree. Spanish moss, or something very like it, festooned the branches and glistened with moisture when she shone the light on it. Around her the nocturnal insects quieted as they heard her approach. She had no qualms about making noise. She wanted Morrainee to know someone was there. But she also wanted her to know that someone was a friend.

With the pencil flash tucked under her arm, she put a finger from each hand to her lips, and whistled in a pitch and volume that sent creatures, presumably avian analogs, flapping into the night sky. The moment was set now; she was on the verge of completing the Rescue that Ellis Darden had wanted to assign her.

"I think you can hear me, Mori," she said conversationally. "The situation in the estate is under control. Poppa is himself again. It's time to come back."

Silence responded.

After a moment, she added, forcing the lie, "Oh, and in case you didn't recognize my voice, it's me, Yoelin."

More silence followed, but she thought to hear a slight rustling up in the tree. She refrained from shining her light up there.

The whisper came, barely audible. "Prove it."

Yoelin relaxed. Whatever happened now, this Rescue would end well.

She laughed, and said, "I'd show you the diamond birthmark on my thigh, but it's really too dark for that."

". . . Yo-Yoelin?"

"Right here in the scratched-up and sodden flesh, with a few denizens crawling up my legs and arms."

Morrainee Thibbony dropped from an overhanging branch to land on her feet a meter away. Yoelin bathed her in what light she could, being careful to avoid shining it directly into her eyes. The girl before her, on the verge of womanhood, was wearing the remains of a green top and denims. Stains of bark and dirt smudged her bare arms, and her hair was a red-orange thicket. Her voice sounded feeble, as if from lack of use.

"You-you're back," she croaked. "You c-came b-back after all these, these years."

"You," said Yoelin, "are a mess." She wrinkled her nose and added, "And when did you bathe last?"

Morrainee sniffled, and hung her head. "Please don't go on at me, Yoey."

The plea and the vaguely-familiar diminutive broke Yoelin. With no choice now except to embrace the jaws of the trap, she held Morrainee as if never to let her go. The girl could not possibly be her sister, but she deserved this moment. Yoelin's hand on the back of the girl's head pressed her face into Yoelin's neck. She felt the girl's lips move, but heard no words. Her neck was wet now, as tears flowed.

The "Yoey" continued to echo through her memories, softly resounding from nowhere, and flowing back full circle. But where had it come from?

Yoelin's mind raced with protests. *I* can't *have a sister, I can't, I* can't. *I can't be Yoey.*

The girl's body racked with sobs, and Yoelin returned to the task at hand, holding her even more tightly. "It's all right now, Mori," she whispered, the words of rescue, words she had breathed on so many other occasions. "It's all right. You're safe now."

"S-s-safe."

"Yes."

She dried her tears on Yoelin's jersey. She leaned back in the circle of Yoelin's arms. After a moment, she said, "And hungry, for something other than nuts and sour fruit. I even ate bugs."

"Why am I not surprised?"

She started to lead the girl back the way she had come, but Morrainee tugged at her arm.

"No, this way," she said, feeling her way in the dark. "We'll come out near the lake, and with fewer scratches. Yoey . . . where have you *been*? What *happened*?"

Yoelin walled off the questions in her mind. "I'd rather not talk about it right now," she said. "There are things I have to figure out. Things I don't understand."

They slipped past night-blooming jasmine, and out onto the glideway that led to the estate.

"That sounds dark," said Morrainee.

"It is. Mori, before we go inside, there are some developments you should be aware of. Delgado is dead, and his—"

"Good," Morrainee said bitterly.

"Right. Most of the people he embedded are dead as well, and the three who remain are now loyal to . . . you're not going to like this, but—"

"Wren. Warren."

Yoelin frowned, incredulous. "You know?"

"I've had a lot of time to think this through, Yoey."

Inwardly Yoelin cringed at the nickname. She just wasn't ready; she could not see herself as ever being ready.

"He was using me to take over," Morrainee went on. "I was afraid, so I ran. I don't know what I thought I was going to do. I had to stay around, in case . . . you know, in case I thought of something. Poppa scarcely knew who I was . . ."

"They were drugging him, Mori. Jonas found out, and put a stop to it. Poppa's much better now, although he does have a lapse or two now and then." At the door, she paused. "Mori, Wren is dead. I killed him."

"Good."

"Morrainee!"

"You taught me that before you left," said Morrainee. "You do what you have to do. I was only five, but I, I never forgot that. No matter how hard . . ." She began to cry again. "I've missed you, Yoey. Sixteen years! Omigod, how I've missed you."

I can't, thought Yoelin. But she hugged the girl, just the same.

Presently the tears and shaking subsided. A tug on the bell rope brought Jonas to the door. His eyes took in everything, though his expression never altered from one of professional efficiency.

"Come in, Miladies," he said, with just the slightest hint of tightness in his voice. "Your father is waiting for you in his office. Meanwhile, I shall awaken the beautician."

"No, don't bother her," said Morrainee, stronger now, and speaking as if in command. "Let her sleep. I'll do with a long shower after I meet with Poppa. Yoey has apprised me of what has transpired this evening and earlier. Tell me, is our family security staff still loyal?"

"It is, Milady," answered Jonas, as he led them toward the office.

"I understand there are perhaps three individuals who are Wr . . . Keller's lackeys." Decisiveness shored up her voice, mildly astonishing Yoelin; the girl was far more resilient than her present appearance suggested. "They are not to leave their rooms. Have guards posted at their doors to enforce this. Yoey or I, or my father, will deal with them in the morning."

"Very good, Milady." He opened the office door and let them pass, closing it behind them.

Aramis Thibbony looked up from the sofa, and snapped to his feet. "There you are, my dear. Are you all right?"

"Thanks to Yoey," she said, and rushed to his arms. "Everything's all right now, Poppa."

Yoelin gazed down at her feet. The Rescue was completed. Ellis Darden could rest easy now. But there remained much unfinished business, much that needed to be cleared up, and she had scant idea how to go about it. Questions were easy—but whom to ask?

Who the hell am I?

You.

She started. "Ellie?" she whispered.

You are who you have made yourself.

"I can't do this, Ellie. I can't be who they think I am."

Let events transpire as they will.

"I don't even know what that means."

"Yoey, who are you talking to?" worried Morrainee.

The corners of her mouth crinkled in frustration. "Myself, Mori. I'm talking to myself. Poppa . . . I have to go."

"No!" cried Morrainee.

Thibbony shook his head. "I need you to run the corporation after I . . . when I can no longer function."

Yoelin found herself trembling. The mere thought of remaining in one place sent a wave of terror coursing throughout her body. But there was more to it: corporate life was a world far different from hers. From that difference the seed of a split with Paul had begun, and it applied here as well. Even though corporate power and influence could protect her from Clewthe, and perhaps even buy her way free from Velanne Moths, corporate life was still a trap.

No, not so much a trap, as a cage. She gave an emphatic shake of her head.

"May I ask why not?" said Thibbony.

Yoelin sighed. She had no good answer for him. "I can't explain right now, I just can't," she said, half-pleading. "I need to . . . get away for a while."

Morrainee grabbed her by the arm and tried to pull her away from the door. "I can't let you go," she wailed. "Not now, not after all these years. Don't leave me!"

Gently Yoelin freed herself. "I promise I will return, Mori. When I do, I'll explain."

She kissed the girl's forehead, and left the office, thumbing tears from her cheeks as she strode toward the front door.

An hour later found Yoelin seated at one of the tables at Hamisi's deli, nibbling at a split bread roll stuffed with cold cuts, with a mug of coffee and a glass of ice water as her choices of beverage. With no other custom to occupy him, Hamisi accepted her invitation to sit with her. At first he kept silent, for which she was grateful; she sought nothing more than some quiet time without the need for thought. Soon enough, thoughts filtered in. She swallowed, and tapped her Palmetto.

The Palmetto blinked: Abnoba's wordless response.

Yoelin wanted to savor the moment, but instead found only a measure of relief. "Abby, reactivate my Guardian Angel and Rescue sites."

"Reactivated." Then, to Yoelin's surprise, voluntarily: *"You have seven queries."*

From across the table, Hamisi looked a question at her.

"It seems I have to go back to work," she told him.

"Rescues."

That's who I am, she thought. *That's what I do.*

She nodded. "Abby, any messages?"

"Dannik Exeter pinged you."

"Raise him, please. Visual, no hologram."

His face and shoulders appeared in the monitor. He still brought to her mind the image of an investment consultant.

"Should I leave?" asked Hamisi.

Yoelin shook her head. "I don't work for him," she said. "If he wants to blurt out classified information, that's on him. Director, what did you want?"

Exeter gave a frosty smile. "Just to remind you that you owe me two favors."

"So I do," she agreed. "But not for a while. I actually have a backlog."

"Understood. Also, the results are in regarding your DNA test."

"I don't want to know," snapped Yoelin, and closed commo before he could add further.

I don't want to know. I can't know.

"Something has happened to you," Hamisi observed. "If you like, I can go to a nearby kiosk for something stronger than water."

"When do you close?" she asked.

"About two more hours."

"I might ask you to stay open longer."

"For you: of course."

She drummed her flat hand on the table top for a few seconds. Finally, her mind made up, she said, "I know a place that needs a deli and someone to manage it. This place could also use a teacher of history. Protection money is not tolerated. I myself am traveling there tomorrow. You and your family are welcome to travel with me. I will arrange lodging for you there, and some funding to get you started."

For long seconds Hamisi simply gazed at her. "This is a Rescue?" he said at last.

"You have been kind and understanding, Hamisi. *Asante*, thank you. Your friendship means more to me than you know. Now, is this what you would like to do?"

Hamisi swallowed hard, and nodded. "A fresh start," he whispered. "A free start."

But Yoelin scarcely heard him. Her attention had been diverted to the center of the Terminal, where a tallish young woman was passing in front of the deli. Yoelin had but a blurred vision of her: short chestnut hair, white blouse with an open brown vest, ankle-length cinnamon skirt like gossamer that swished around her legs as she walked. She was wearing black lip gloss, and her features were heavily mascaraed. Arabesques in dark henna decorated her bare forearms and hands.

But what had captured Yoelin's attention was the way she walked. There was something almost predatory about it. Now, as she passed, she turned her face toward the deli, just for a moment, not breaking stride. Seconds later she merged with a small clot of late-night shoppers, and out of sight.

"And that hasn't been resolved, either," whispered Yoelin, to herself. "Has it."

Hamisi tilted his head at her, uncertain.

"I have . . . something I need to address," she told him, the hint gentle. "And perhaps you have something to pack for your trip."

*

Half an hour passed. Yoelin finished the bread roll and accepted a refill of her coffee mug. At her instruction, Hamisi prepared a second mug and set it across the table from her, before backing away.

Her eyes catching the motion of an approach, Yoelin looked up. Jonas, still dressed as a butler, sat down in the chair appointed by the second coffee mug. Crossing his arms on the table, he leaned slightly forward, waiting to learn the reason for her request to meet with him.

Yoelin tapped her Palmetto twice, the signal for it to begin recording.

"Thank you for coming, Jonas," she said.

"Of course, Mi . . . *M'selle.*"

Still Yoelin hesitated. She had Rescues to perform, but she also had questions that needed answers. A little here and a little there, and perhaps one day she might learn much of the truth.

She took a deep breath, and gave herself a tiny nod.

"Jonas," she said. "I want you now to regard me as ignorant. Amnesiac, if you like."

"I will try, *M'selle.*"

"Thank you. Now tell me everything—and I do mean everything—you know about Yoelin Thibbony."

THE END

Yoelin Thibbony will return!

Check out all of the Nomadic Delirium Press titles at:
http://nomadicdeliriumpress.com/blog/shop

Feel free to visit our blog and share your opinions about this book. You can also keep up on future Nomadic Delirium Press releases:
http://nomadicdelirium.wordpress.com/

If you've liked what you've read, please become a patron for Nomadic Delirium Press at
https://www.patreon.com/nomadicdeliriumpress

www.ingramcontent.com/pod-product-compliance
Lightning Source LLC
Chambersburg PA
CBHW051515170626
46811CB00002B/841